Her Love Did Not Change With What Had To Be Done

by

Larry V. Johnson

Larry's Books
Rabun County (Clayton), Georgia

ISBN- 13: 978 - 1500504649

ISBN- 10: 1500504645

DEDICATED

TO MY FOUR SISTERS, CATHERINE, SHIRLEY, ELAINE, LINDA, MY LATE BROTHER, WAYNE, MY LATE SISTER WANDA, AND MY SISTER-IN-LAW, SHARON

ALL OF THEM HAVE BEEN A TREMENDOUS SUPPORT TO ME THROUGHOUT MY LIFE

CONTENTS

Section One

Fifteen Years Earlier

Section Two

Section Three

Her Love Did Not Change With What Had To Be Done

<u>Including</u>:
**Celeste And The Tall Stranger At 'The Rock'
And
The Opposite Sides Of The Coin**

PREFACE

This story has been divided into three sections. The first section deals with the trauma associated with how a family can be torn apart by one family member. No one suspected what a family member was going to do ...not even the other family members. This section also deals with <u>the first of three murders</u> that happened over a two year period in <u>real life</u> in a Georgia city. Section two covers Celeste and her romance with the 'Tall Stranger' at 'The Rock.' In the third section on 'The Opposite Sides Of The Coin," <u>two</u> more murders occur over the remainder of the two year <u>time</u> period. Were all three murders committed by the same person, or were they done by different individuals? What was the method or weapon used to murder the three victims? How were Courtney and Celeste involved in a dramatic courtroom drama that nearly destroyed their sibling relationship? Both of them battled each other to help save or <u>not</u> help save a loved one from the death penalty. Also, see how Celeste's love for an individual could not change because she knew she had to do what needed to be done.

Read the story and find out more about what happened in these exciting scenes. Even though all three murders happened in <u>real life</u>, the courtroom scenes are <u>strictly fictional</u>. Scenes and names have been changed to protect those who were involved.

Section One

Introducing <u>Emily Mae Zetterower</u>

Why she left was very mysterious

<u>Notes</u>:

Some of the information in the following <u>scenarios</u> happened in <u>two</u> Georgia cities. The exact geographical area as to where the incidents happened has been changed to New York to protect those who were involved. Also, the scenes of Emily leaving Randy happened in real life. In addition, all three murders happened over a two year period in real life.

It was another beautiful Saturday morning at Westonia Island, New York just across the bay from Janelle's Vineyard. Emily Mae Zetterower and her husband Randy Allen Zetterower were sleeping in their beautiful queen-size bed. Emily woke up and looked over at the clock on the night stand. It was 6:09 A.M. This was earlier than the time of 6:30 A.M. that she had set the night before for the alarm to wake her up that morning. Even though she had awakened before 6:30 A. M., she decided that it was time for her to get up, get dressed, have coffee and a piece of toast, and leave home as quickly as possible before Randy who was still asleep woke up. She had some business that she wanted to take care of before she opened 'Aunt Emily's

Steak and Pizza House' that she owned. Usually on Saturday, she did not open the restaurant for business until 10:30 A.M. just before the lunch hour. She knew that if Randy woke up before she left he would question her as to why she was leaving, or why she was going to the restaurant so early. Emily told herself that no one needed to know what she was going to be doing before opening the restaurant …and especially not Randy.

As Emily was getting out of bed, the whistle of a train could be heard from the railroad that was about three hundred feet over the hill behind them. Emily was thankful that Randy was not awakened by the train that came through the area at 6:10 A.M. She eased out of bed and put her feet into her bedroom slippers. Then, she glanced back at Randy. He had not even moved a muscle. During the time that she had been married to him she knew he could sleep through anything. That aspect of his life proved to be useful in a big way to Emily on this particular morning.

Emily looked over at Randy with a <u>cold look</u> on her face. As she turned away from looking at him, she said to herself that it would not be long before it would be over. Emily walked into their private bath room, removed her skimpy sheer baby doll PJs, took a shower in the beautiful garden tub, got dressed and went into the kitchen to have a cup of coffee. The coffee maker was automatic. So, after the coffee was fixed in the coffee maker and the timer was set the night before, it was ready the next morning. Usually, she would drink, at least, two cups of coffee every morning. On this particular morning after drinking her first cup, she decided she would prepare a big delicious breakfast for herself…one like she had never prepared before. She wanted to eat at home this morning with Courtney and Celeste before going to take care of some important business early that morning before she opened her restaurant at 10:30 A.M. So she had asked each one of them to set their clocks the night before to get up at 6:30 A.M. ...the same time that she had planned to get up that morning.

Within minutes before 6:30 A.M., Emily's youngest eight year old daughter, Celeste, came through the kitchen door on the side that went to Celeste and Courtney's bedrooms. She looked toward her mom at the same time that her mom looked toward her, and said, "Good morning mom." "Good morning Celeste," said Emily. "Did you sleep good last night?" "Yes, but I had a crazy dream. I do not know if I should share it with anyone; but something happened in it that cause me to wake up at 4 A.M., and I could not go back to sleep. Since I was awake from then until now, I reached over from my bed to the clock on the night stand and turned off the alarm before it went off at 6:30 A.M. which was the time that I promised you that I would meet you this morning in the kitchen.

Celeste walks over to the refrigerator, takes the big jar of orange juice out, and pours it in a glass that she gets from the cabinet. She also gets a strawberry 'turn-over' from the pantry and puts it in the small oven. Within minutes of the time that she gets a glass of orange juice and the warmed-over strawberry 'turn-over,' she joins her mother who is now sitting at the small dinette table in the kitchen. She looks at her mother, and says, "I feel that I need to share my dream with you." Her mother says, "Okay. I'd like to hear about it. But, try to be brief because I have some very important business that I need to take care of this morning." Celeste began, and said, "I dreamed about a family that appeared to be very happy together; but the happiness was torn apart by one of the family members. That family member was involved in an incident that affected the others in the family in a very big and devastating manner. I dream dreams all of the time, and I usually do not let the bad ones bother me. But, last week I was talking to my Science teacher at school. At one point in our conversation, the subject of dreams and their meaning was mentioned. She told me that she believed some dreams have a meaning or they are

3

there to warn the person who has the dream about something that is going to happen in his/her life. In my dream, I saw a family member leave home to be with another person. I do not believe that it would be me or my older sister, Karen. That only leaves you and dad. But that is enough of my crazy dream. I need to eat my strawberry 'turn-over' while it is still at least warm," said Celeste.

Notes:

Celeste's brief version about her dream, which ran parallel and coincided with what Emily was going to do in real life in a few hours, caused Emily to go into a state of denial. So, she does not let what she is going to do later affect her conscience. She proceeds with her thoughts to carry out her plans and does not let nothing or anyone interfere with them.

Emily tries to maintain her composure as she says to herself that she cannot believe that Celeste has indirectly just described what she is actually going to do in a few hours.

At that point, Emily looks toward the hallway that leads to Courtney and Celeste's bedrooms, and said, "I guess Courtney forgot to set her alarm to go off at 6:30 A.M. this morning." Celeste responded, and said, "Yes, she probably just forgot."

Then Emily excuses herself and said to Celeste, "As I told you earlier, I have some important business to take care of today." Emily got up from her chair, went over to Celeste, kissed her on the forehead, and said, "Have a great day!" Celeste said, "You have a great day too, mom." Then Emily picked up her purse and a small windbreaker coat that she had put on the sofa and walked out the front door of their home.

Randy wakes up at the sound of Emily's <u>Thunderbird</u> car leaving the house

Just as Emily was backing out of the drive way into the side street in front of their house, Randy wakes up. He looks over and sees that Emily was not in bed next to him. He gets up, puts his pants on, and quickly runs to one of the bedroom windows next to the driveway where he had heard the sound of a car engine. At that point Emily was just backing into the street that was in front of their home. As Randy looks out of the bedroom window, he recognized that it was Emily's car that was backing out of the driveway. Emily put the gear shift of her car 'in drive' and very quickly drove away from their home.

Randy ran into the kitchen where Celeste was still finishing her breakfast, and said, "Do you know where your mother is going this time of the morning ...especially this early on a Saturday morning?" "No dad. I am sorry. But she only told me that she had some important business to take care of today." I guess we will find out later said Randy. She may have wanted to surprise us about something. Then Randy started thinking, and said, "I do not see that any of us have a birthday, and it is not your mother and my wedding anniversary. So, it has to be something else that she is doing today."

At that point, Courtney, their ten year old daughter, walked into the kitchen, and asked the same question that Randy had just asked about where her mother was going and said, "Why did mother leave in such a hurry? I looked out of my bedroom window and saw her driving down the street." "It seems that none of us know what is going on," said Randy. Before Randy could say anymore, Celeste said, "Courtney, you were supposed to get up at 6:30 A.M. and be with your mother and me here in the kitchen before she left." "I remember now," said Courtney. But I forgot to set my alarm clock before going to bed last night. After Courtney made that comment, she got a blueberry 'turn-over' from the refrigerator and put it in the small oven on the countertop.

Notes:

Randy was upset with Emily because he was not included in her plans for him to have breakfast with her, Courtney and Celeste that Saturday morning before she left. He also wondered why Courtney and Celeste did not say anything to him about Emily wanting to have breakfast with them that Saturday morning. They did not say one word to him about the breakfast. Randy wondered why they did not even mention it.

Notes:

Courtney and Celeste did not say anything to Randy about them having breakfast early that Saturday morning with Emily because they thought that she had already told Randy on the Friday night before that Emily wanted everyone to be together for a special reason that Emily did not disclose to anyone in the family.

During the time that Courtney and Celeste had been talking, Randy decided to talk to the girls about what he had been thinking in regard to Emily not inviting him to the breakfast, too. He looked at both girls, and said, "I wonder why she only wanted see both of you before she left. Apparently, she did not want me to know something that she was going to do. So, she left without telling me anything. She should have waked me up. But she did not. Something strange is going on, and I wished that I knew more about it." Then Randy said, "I think that I will call her on her cell phone." When Emily saw that it was Randy calling, she did not answer her phone. Randy told the girls, "She did not answer. I'll try the restaurant." He tried to call the restaurant. No one answered.

Has She Left Him?

On that same Saturday, he was going to help <u>Frank Earl Eubanks</u>
Randy and Emily had met Frank and Sherry <u>eleven years</u> earlier in the same neighborhood

Randy looked at the girls, and said, "I need to go get a shower and go help Frank build a small building today that he needs for his work." "Okay," said Courtney.

<u>Notes</u>:

Eleven years earlier, when Randy and Emily moved into Blue Surf Estates in Westonia Island, New York, they became friends with many of their neighbors. One of the couples that they especially enjoyed being with were Frank and his wife, Sherry. Over those eleven years, Randy and Emily had developed a close relationship with them, and at times they did things together on Saturdays. Now, on this same Saturday that Emily had mysteriously left that morning, Randy was going to help Frank Earl Eubanks build a small building for Frank's tools and various types of machinery related to his job. Randy and Frank had discussed earlier the plans to build the building earlier that week.

When Randy left the kitchen to go take a shower, Celeste finished eating her strawberry 'turn-over' and drinking her glass of orange juice. Courtney took her blueberry 'turn-over' from the small oven, went to the refrigerator, took the gallon of milk out and poured a glass full of milk into a glass that she had gotten from a kitchen cabinet. Then, she joined Celeste at the small kitchen table. At that point, during their casual conversation, Celeste did not mention to Courtney about her dream that she had the night before. They stayed at the small kitchen table and talked about casual things in their everyday life.

After Randy got his shower and put on his work clothes, he came back into the kitchen where Courtney and Celeste were still sitting at the small kitchen table relaxing and enjoying each other's company. They looked up at him when he entered the room. Randy approached the table, and said, "Before I leave to go to Frank's home, I need to know if you two still want to go to your mother's restaurant with me today at noon time when I take my break from helping Frank. You may have changed your mind after your mother and I discussed it with you last night ...especially since she left us this morning. Do you two still feel like going to the restaurant at noon time with me, or have you changed your mind?" Both girls gave an affirmative, "We have not changed our minds. Yes, we want to go." Then Courtney said, "We want to be there with you when mother tells you why she left us this morning." "Okay," said Randy. "I'll pick you two up at twelve noon. Maybe when we I talk to her when we go to the restaurant at lunch time we can all get some answers about why she left. So, "I guess we will just have to wait until we see her then." Randy walked to the front door of their home, opened the door, closed it behind him, and got in his car to go to Frank's house.

A few days earlier, before this particular Saturday, Randy had asked Frank if he and his wife Sherry would join him and his daughters Courtney and Celeste at Emily's 'Aunt Emily's Steak and Pizza House,' for their lunch break on that Saturday at noon time. During that brief conversation, Randy told them that Emily would be there, and they could all have lunch together.

Notes:

Even though Emily had left Randy, Courtney, and Celeste earlier that morning without saying anything to them about where she was going, they still looked forward to seeing her at noon time. Usually, Emily would take time from her busy schedule at the restaurant to join Randy and the girls each Saturday unless they had something else planned ...which was not too often since they wanted to spend this time with her.

As Randy drove the short drive toward Frank's house, he told himself that he was going to ask Emily in a diplomatic way why she left earlier that morning when he saw her later that day. Some of the thoughts that came to his mind centered on how he needed to approach her in regard to the issue of why she left. He knew that he was going to have to be very tactful in what he said because he loved her and did not want to cause or create any dissention between them.

She shared it with Courtney

Later that same Saturday morning after Randy went to help his friend, Frank, build a small building, Celeste shared her dream with her older sister, Courtney Anne. After she shared the same dream to Courtney that she had told Emily, Celeste said, "Mother acted very strange after I told her about the dream. "I hope it does not involve her," said Celeste. "I hope it does not either," said Karen. "I did not want to say anything to dad about the dream and how it seemed to affect mom," said Celeste. "I'm glad that you did not, too," said Karen.

It is a challenge to get it out of his mind

When Randy started working with Frank that Saturday morning, Frank noticed that Randy was not his 'happy-go-lucky' self that he usually exhibited most of the time. Frank said, "Is everything okay?" "Everything is fine," said Randy. "Well really it isn't. Emily left home this morning and did not tell anyone where she was going." "She did not even give you a hint," said Frank. "No not at all except it did cross my mind that she may be going to the restaurant to take care of some important business before it opened this morning. But, if she was not going to the restaurant, I just hope everything else in her life is okay. I do not think it involves our relationship because things have been going good between us." Frank turned to face Randy, and said, "She will probably tell you about why she left when we see her for lunch today at the restaurant." "Well, I hope so," said Randy. "She has always come home to be with me and the girls every evening. So, I will wait to see what she says."

Frank hesitated for a moment as he continued looking toward Randy. Then he changed the tone of the conversation as he said, "Randy, I remember when Sherry and I met you and Emily eleven years ago when you moved to Blue Surf Estates here in Westonia." "Yes, I remember it, too." Since that time we have thoroughly enjoyed both you and Sherry's friendship, and we look forward to continuing to enjoy that friendship with you and Sherry for many years to come. Randy knew that the conversation needed to terminate so that they could get the job of building the small house in one day. So, he quickly got his thoughts together and centered his attention on the project that he and Frank were doing.

Before Randy and Frank knew it the morning had passed by quickly. They had about half of their work done at that point. Randy looked at Frank, and said, "Courtney and Celeste are going with us to the restaurant today. I am going to my house and pick them up. I'll meet you there in about thirty minutes." "Okay," said Frank. Frank called Sherry on her cell phone; but could not get her. When she did not answer her phone, he told himself that they had already talked about meeting each other, Randy and the girls at 12 noon at the restaurant. So, he said to himself that he would see her there. When Frank arrived just before noon, he did not see Sherry anywhere. Within a few minutes, Randy and the girls joined Frank. Frank looked at Randy, and said, "I'm sorry that Sherry is not here yet. She is always on time for everything that we do. So, she should be here shortly."

As Randy, Frank, Courtney, and Celeste approached the door to the restaurant, Frank's cell phone rang. It was Sherry. She said, "I am sorry. But, I won't be able to join you, Randy, and the girls. I had a 'beauty' appointment this morning that I had to break. The only other opening that was available today was 12 noon." "Okay," said Frank. "I miss you." "I miss you, too," said Sherry. Then they both said, "Good bye," and turned off their cell phones. Frank turned toward Randy and the girls, and said, "It looks like Sherry won't be joining us for lunch." "That is okay," said Randy.

Emily was <u>not</u> in the restaurant
Sherry did not join them
The manager leaves in a hurry

Randy, Frank, and the girls walked into Emily's 'Aunt Emily's Steak and Pizza House' ...where breakfast was also served six days a week. They did not see Emily anywhere. Randy went to the back of the restaurant, and did not see her there. When Randy could not find Emily he went to the head waitress, Betty, whom he knew. Betty knew that Randy was Emily's husband and she also knew Courtney and Celeste because they had been in many times before. Randy and Betty said, "Hello" to each other. Then Betty and both girls exchanged greetings. Randy looked over at Frank, and introduced her to Frank. Frank and Betty exchanged introduction greetings. Then, Randy asked

Betty, "Have you seen Emily today?" "No, Emily has not come in this morning. "Has she called?" "No, she has not called either. She hired a new man to run the restaurant just yesterday. His name is Jim." "I'd like to meet him," said Randy. Betty said, "He is not here. Just after I placed your order, he said that he had to leave to take care of some urgent business. I am sorry." "That is okay," said Randy.

Notes:

Jim had left the restaurant quickly when he saw that Randy, Frank, and the girls had come into the restaurant. It also made him nervous when he overhead Randy inquiring about why Emily was not there. He did not want to discuss anything relating to her with Randy.

Randy, Frank, Courtney, and Celeste ate their lunch. Then, Randy took the girls back home. Just as the girls were getting out of his car in their driveway next to the house, Randy said to the girls, "If your mother comes home before I leave Frank's home, call me on my cell phone." "We sure will call you when she comes home," said Courtney. After Courtney and Celeste entered their home, Randy drove back to Frank's place to finish the building project.

Later, that afternoon, after Randy and Frank had completed the building project, Frank thanked Randy for helping him build the building. Then Randy said, "I cannot wait until Emily comes home this afternoon or evening so that Courtney, Celeste, and I can find out why she left home so earlier this morning ...and also why she was not at the restaurant today.

They were disturbed when she did not come home that evening

When Randy came home from working with Frank at 5:30, he expected to see Emily; but she had not returned. He went down the hall of the girl's bedrooms and knocked on the door to Karen's room. She said, "Come in." Randy walked in with a gloomy facial expression. By the way that he looked at her, Karen knew that he was going to ask about Emily, and said, "No, I have not seen nor heard from her." As Randy went back into the living room, sat on the sofa, and turned on TV to watch the news, Celeste came in and said, "I am worried about mother." Then Randy said, "I do not know what to think. Usually she is always home in the evenings or she calls to let us know if she is going to be late." Randy, Karen, and Celeste waited for two hours which turned into six. At 11:30, Randy insisted that the girls go to bed. He said, "If this had been a school night rather than a Saturday evening, you would have needed to be in bed by 9 P.M." All three said, "Good night to each other, went into their separate bedrooms, and went to bed.

Larry V. Johnson

Will She Return?

<u>Notes</u>:

The following scenario happened in <u>real life</u> in a small Georgia city.

On that same Saturday afternoon, when Randy and Frank had finished building the small tool and machine house that Frank needed, Frank's wife Sherry came home from shopping for groceries and getting her hair done at the 'Beauty Palace." Both Frank and Sherry exchanged greetings and inquired about how their day had been. Then Sherry briefly kissed Frank on his lips, and said, "Why don't we go out for pizza tonight." "Okay," said Frank. "I have not had one in a while." Frank and Sherry left home and went out to eat at 'Mama's Pizza House.' On the way home after eating a big fifteen inch pizza together, Frank said, "Randy is worried about Emily. He said that she left home this morning and did not tell anyone where she was going. That does not sound like Emily. According to Randy, she always tells them what she is going to do when she leaves the house." Sherry said, "I'm sorry that she left."

She reveals it
Is she gone permanently?

Later, that evening, after watching a movie on TV, Frank and Sherry got ready to go to bed at about 11:45 that Saturday night. Just as Frank was getting into bed next to her, Sherry sat up, and said, "There is something that I need to tell you." "Last Saturday, when I went to the grocery store, I saw Emily. We talked for a few moments. During our brief conversation, Emily said, "I have something that I need to tell you; but I do not want to share it with you here." Then I told her, "Let's shop together now and then go to the 'Doughnut Shoppe' where we can talk." Emily responded to me, and said, "Okay. That sounds like a good idea."

Sherry continued, and said, "For the next few minutes we shopped for the things that we needed. After shopping together at the grocery store, Emily and I went out to get some coffee and a doughnut at the 'Doughnut Shoppe.' While there she shared something with me that she did not want anyone knowing about." The look that Sherry had on her face and by the way that she was looking at him, Frank knew that it had to do with Emily leaving Randy and the girls that Saturday Morning. So he said, "Okay." Sherry continued, and said, "Emily told me about how she was going to leave Randy, Courtney, and Celeste to go and be with Jim Al Benefer next Saturday ...which was today." "It is not that I do not believe you; but it is hard to comprehend that she would leave her loving husband, Randy, and her two daughters, Courtney Anne Zetterower, and Celeste Jane Zetterower to be with Jim," said Frank. "I know," said Sherry. "I could not believe it either. She made me promise that I would not say anything to anyone about it until after she left them to be with Jim. So, that is why I have not even told you about what she was going to do earlier today." "That is okay," said Frank. "I know that you like to keep your promise to someone who has confided in you."

Notes:

Earlier in the week, Emily had already told Sherry, "I am going to leave my husband, Randy Jake Zetterower, my two daughters, Courtney Anne Zetterower, and Celeste Jane

Zetterower next Saturday to be with Jim Al Benefer whom I met while in high school. I also want you to understand that Jim and I are not going to be living together. Over the last few weeks each one of us found a separate place to stay until I get a divorce from Randy and Jim and I get married."

When Emily shared this information with Sherry on a 'friend to friend confidant' basis, she asked Sherry to keep quiet about it until after she carried out her plans to be with Jim. Even though Sherry was surprised about what Emily was going to do, she did not want to say anything against it because what she would say in a negative manner could probably hurt their friendship. So, in a supportive manner, she said, "Okay, if that is what you feel like you need to do." Then Emily said, "Promise me that you will not say anything to anyone about what I have told you ...not even your husband, Frank." "I promise you that I will not reveal anything to anyone about what you have told me ...not even my husband," said Sherry.

Notes:

Therefore, Sherry knew earlier that Emily was going to leave Randy and the girls; but she did not tell anyone. She did not even share it with her husband, Frank. So, he did not know anything about it either.

Frank looked at the clock on the night stand, and said, "Even though it is late, I think I need to call Randy and tell him now. He will be very upset when he finds out that she has left him and even more upset if I do not call him now and tell him rather than wait until in the morning." "I agree," said Sherry.

The shock of finding out

Frank dialed Randy's phone number. Randy had just begun to get sleepy after he went to bed at 11:30 P.M. It was now 11:59 P.M. Randy looked at the caller-ID and saw that it was Frank calling. He said, "Hello." Frank said, "I hope I did not wake you; but I have something important to tell you …probably something that you may not want to hear." "Okay, go ahead," said Randy. "Sherry has just revealed to me why Emily left this morning." At this point Randy was wide awake. He said, "Go ahead, I am listening." Frank hesitated, and very carefully said, "Emily has made the decision to leave you and the girls and go to be with Jim Al Benefer." Randy was in shock and waited for a moment as he got himself together. With tears in his eyes, he said, "I never would have suspected it. I thought that Emily and I had a wonderful marriage and nothing or nobody could take away the great relationship that I thought we had together. At that point Randy said, "Let me go and see if Courtney and Celeste are awake. If they are awake, I want them to listen on their phones and hear what you have to say. Since I now know why Emily did not return this evening, they may never forgive me if I did not tell them immediately when I found out." "I think that would be a good idea," said Frank. "I'll be back in a minute." "Okay," said Frank.

Randy knocked on both of the girl's bedroom doors. Each one was still disturbed about their mother not coming home to the point that neither one of them could go to sleep. Both of them came to their doors and opened them. Randy stood in the hall in front of the open doors to each bedroom, and said, "Frank, the man that I worked with today and whom you both know has some information regarding your mother. He has been telling me why she left this past Saturday. I want you to get on the phones that are in each of your bedrooms and listen to what he has to say. I know that it is after midnight. But, I thought that you needed to know about why your mother left now rather than wait until in the morning for me to tell you."

Both, Courtney and Celeste were wondering what Frank was going to say. They could not imagine what was 'going on' …especially since it involved their mother. Randy walked back to the phone in his bedroom, and said, "Frank, I'm back. I have

Courtney and Celeste on their extension phones. Are you all there?" "Yes we are dad," said the girls in unison. Randy wanted the girls to know what Frank had told him at the beginning of the conversation before they got on their extension phones. So, he asked Frank to briefly repeat what he had told him at the beginning of the conversation. After Frank went over the initial part of the conversation that Randy had already heard, more tears came into Randy's eyes. Both girls were in tears, too. Randy got his emotions together, and said, "I remember Jim. I think Emily wanted to date him when they were in high school, but he never seemed interested enough to want to ask her out." Then Frank continued, and said, "Sherry also told me that Emily has been keeping in contact with Jim since all three of you got out of high school." "I thought that I knew her," said Randy. "But, I don't guess I did." "We never know," said Frank. As frank continued, he said, "Jim was incarcerated for embezzlement at the bank where he worked about three years ago. He has now served his time and was released from prison last month."

Randy was silent for a moment. The girls were also quiet. It seemed that everyone was in a 'state-of-shock.' After the short period of silence from everyone including Frank, Courtney spoke up and said, "Dad, are you okay?" "Yes, I am going to be okay," said Randy. Then both girls broke down and cried. At that time neither one could grasp what they had heard. Both of them loved their mother and never dreamed that this would ever happen. They could not believe that it was real. It seemed like a dream.

Throughout the conversation between Frank and Randy, Sherry had been listening to them on her and Frank's 'speaker-phone.' She did not say a word; but just listened. At the point where Courtney was asking Randy if he was okay, Sherry decided that she wanted to add more to the story. She felt that she needed to tell them why she had to reschedule her 'beauty' appointment and not have lunch with them this past Saturday. So, she interrupted Frank as he was talking to Randy

19

and the girls, and said, "There is something else that I need to tell everyone." "Okay," said Frank. "Emily wanted me to meet with her this <u>past</u> Saturday morning shortly after she left her home and shortly after she talked to Jim to tell me that she was <u>not</u> going to be in the restaurant too often anymore. She was going to let Jim take over and manage it for her. That was where I was this past Saturday morning when I had to cancel my 'beauty' appointment and reschedule it for 12 noon when I was supposed to meet all of you at the restaurant." "Now, we all know," said Frank. Randy and the girls were very distraught when Sherry said what she did. They still could not believe what Emily had done and was continuing to do in the decision that she had made to leave them. Then, Sherry said, "I have one more thing to say, "I do not know why Emily did not call me from where she was with Jim and tell me over the phone about her not being in the restaurant too often anymore. She could have called me then and told me about it rather than meet me at the 'Birdsong Building' where we met."

Notes:

Sherry had talked to Emily earlier that morning when they met in the 'Birdsong Building.' That was why she had to break her appointment with the 'Beauty Shoppe' that morning and reschedule it for the noon time hour. She also knew that Emily would not be at the restaurant for their lunch hour.

In the conversation, Emily told Sherry that everything had gone according to her plans. Then she said, "I plan to have Randy served with divorce papers later this week. Then Jim and I can get married." Sherry said, "Okay." That was the only comment that she could make under the circumstances. Usually, at another time Sherry would have said, "Congratulations." But she did not say it this time. Emily could sense that Sherry was tense about what she had told Sherry; but, since they were friends, she did not mention it.

All the time that Frank was talking to Randy, Sherry was still listening quietly on their 'speaker-phone.' She did not say anything else ...not even one word. During the remainder of the conversation between Frank, Randy, Courtney, and Celeste, Sherry began to feel remorseful; but she told herself that she had made a promise to Emily not to tell anyone until after it all happened ...which was now. So she started thinking thoughts that helped her maintain a comfortable demeanor as she listened in on Frank and Randy's continued conversation about the situation. Throughout the remainder of their conversation Sherry did not feel any sense of remorse at all because she felt that she had kept her promise to Emily who was still her good friend.

Just before Frank was concluding his call to Randy, Frank apologized to him for Sherry not sharing the information about what Emily was going to do on that Saturday. He said, "According to Sherry, she promised Emily that she would not say anything to anyone that she was leaving you, Courtney, and Celeste yesterday morning." Then he said, "Randy, if there is anything that I can do to help you let me know." "I will," said Randy. Everyone exchanged 'good byes' and hung up their phones.

Frank looked over at Sherry ...who was still silent. She still did not say a word. Even though Sherry had promised Emily that she would not reveal to anyone that Emily was leaving Randy and the girls, Frank was very upset with her. But, he did not want to hurt his marriage. So, he did not say anymore to Sherry about her not revealing what Emily was going to do that previous Saturday.

Notes:

It was now <u>past midnight</u> and the beginning of Sunday the day after that hurtful incident of Emily leaving Randy and the two girls.

No one suspected that Emily was going to leave Randy, Courtney, and Celeste. Even though Celeste had a dream on the Friday night prior to the Saturday that Emily left, Celeste did not realize that it was really going to happen. On Sunday morning, after Sherry told Frank that Emily would not be back, Courtney approached Celeste, and said, "Your dream was 'for real.'" "I know, and I cannot believe it," said Celeste.

Also, even though Sherry had shared information about Emily making plans to leave Randy and the girls, she did not let them know that she knew Emily was going to have Randy served with divorce papers later that week so that she could leave him and marry Jim.

She left and wanted a divorce

He is devastated and shocked when served with the divorce papers

The girls are in 'a state of disbelief'

One evening after Randy came home from work, the door bell rang. Randy went to the front door and opened it. There was a man standing at the door with papers in his hand. The man said, "Are you Mr. Randy Zetterower?" "Yes I am," said Randy. "I am here to serve you with these papers." He handed Randy the papers, and said, "Have a good evening." Then he left. Randy closed the door as Courtney and Celeste came into the living room. Both of them said together, "Who was that dad?" "I don't know; but he gave me these papers." Randy briefly looked over the papers that he had in his hand. He saw that they were from Emily's attorney, and they stated that she wanted a divorce from him. When he told Courtney and Celeste about what was in the papers, both of them screamed, "Oh no! She cannot do this to us." "I afraid so," said Randy.

Everyone knew about the divorce
It did not affect her restaurant business

Emily develops a great reputation for having one of the best restaurants in the country. Both the food and the service from the waitresses were of very high quality. When it was discovered through the media of TV, radio, and newspapers about her divorcing Randy, it did not hurt her business at all. In fact, the publicity created more business. People from all over the country came to enjoy her excellent food and the good service from the waitresses.

When people found out that she was divorcing Randy, it did not affect her business. In fact, the publicity made it better.

He wanted to ask her why

Randy wanted to talk to Emily about the situation. He was still 'in the dark' about why she had left and about why she wanted to divorce him. On the following Monday, he made plans to go by the restaurant to talk to her. He went in the afternoon so that he could take Courtney and Celeste with him when they were out of school.

When they arrived at the restaurant, Randy talked to Betty, the same waitress that he talked to when he came into the restaurant on the previous Saturday. She said, "Emily has not been here today." Then Randy asked to speak to, Jim, the new manager. The waitress went to check and see if he was available. She came back, and said, "He is very busy at the moment. It may be a few minutes before he can see you." "That is fine," said Randy. Then the waitress said, "I can take your order while you wait." "Well, I had not planned to eat anything when I came by. But, since I am here, and I am sure the girls are hungry because they always get snacks when they come home from school, we will place an order." Randy ordered a deluxe hamburger and hash browns to go with it Then, he ask for sweet Tea to drink. The girls liked what he had ordered, and they got the same thing. But, for their drink they ordered pink lemonade instead of sweet Tea.

The First Murder

Within minutes after Randy and the girls had placed their order, Betty brings their food to them on a tray. She places Courtney and Celeste's food in front of each one of them. Then she takes Randy's hamburger, hash browns, and sweet Tea and puts them in front of him. As each one enjoys the food, Randy said, "This is the best hamburger that I have ever eaten. It is delicious and the hash browns are good too." The girls make similar comments about each of their hamburgers.

After Randy has taken several bites of his hamburger and eats some of his hash browns he begins to feel a little nauseated. He feels like he is going to vomit. Quickly he drinks some of his Tea. But that does not help. Randy lets out a low groaning sound and grabs his stomach with his right hand, and throws up blood as his head falls over into his plate. Then his body fell out of the chair at the restaurant table and folds up on the floor. Just as Randy's body was falling to the floor, both Courtney and Celeste threw up in their plates. They wiped their mouths with the big table cloth, stood up from the table, and go over to check on their dad. As they looked at him, they saw that his eyes had rolled back into their eye sockets. Randy, Courtney, and Celeste's waitress, Betty, saw Randy's body fall over from his chair. She grabbed the hand-held restaurant phone from its charging cradle on the counter next to the cash register and rushed over to where the girls were now standing over Randy lying on the floor. She immediately dials 911. Within minutes, the local police and paramedics of Westonia Island, New York

25

were there. When the police and paramedics arrived at the restaurant, the paramedics examined Randy. One of the paramedics Jerome Hendricks looked over at Courtney and Celeste, and asked, "Is this your dad?" "Yes, he is my dad," said Courtney. Then she said, "Is he going to be okay." Then Jerome sighed, and said, "I am sorry, but he won't be with us anymore. "Surely, you aren't saying he is dead," said Celeste. He was too healthy with no medical problems." Once again the paramedic, Jerome, said, "I am so sorry." Celeste was next to Courtney when Jerome was talking to Courtney. After hearing the dreadful news, Courtney and Celeste went into a state-of-shock to the point that both of them lose their voices and could not talk for a few moments. Courtney motioned for Celeste to follow her. Both of them walked over to another table close by the one where they were eating their meal. They pulled out two chairs at the table and sat down.

Within minutes after Courtney and Celeste had lost their voice as a result of the traumatic experience about Randy being pronounced dead in the restaurant, one of the two police officers, Officer David Morgan, who were there at the scene walked over to Courtney at the table, and said, "I'd like to ask you some questions." At that point Courtney could speak again. So she said, "Okay." Officer Morgan said, "Was Randy taking any kind of medicine on a regular basis or was he under a doctor's care for a medical reason?" Officer Morgan continued, and said, "Do you know if he had any illness lately that may have been terminal?" Courtney said, "In response to what you have asked me, "I am sorry; but I do not have any knowledge about any of those questions regarding my dad." "Okay," said Officer Morgan. "Thanks for taking the time to talk with me. I know that your dad's death has been hard on you and Celeste. I may be talking to you again, soon." "Okay," said Courtney. Celeste was listening to the entire conversation between Officer Morgan and Courtney; but she did not say a word until after Officer Morgan left. Then she said, "Courtney, why did he have to ask you those questions now?" "I think that was very inconsiderate of him to put you into a time of interrogation …especially this soon after what we have been through with dad's death." "I know said Courtney. But it seems that some people just do not think like they should under certain circumstances." "Yes! You are right," said Celeste.

Many of the customers in the restaurant thought that Randy had a health problem and had just passed out …until he was pronounced dead. When they found out that Randy was dead, some of them became panicky while others become hysterical and scream. Officer Laura Latham and Officer Ben Kostern, the two police officers who were there, tried to keep everyone calm and maintain order as best that they could under the circumstances. Courtney and Celeste broke into sobs and tears. Still in disbelief about what had happened, the officers ask to speak to the manager, Jim. Betty, the waitress said that he had to leave on an emergency involving his daughter who had been in the hospital for the last two days.

Officer Latham, one of the police officers, who had come to investigate what had happened to Randy at the restaurant and also keep order among the restaurant patrons called the Westonia Island Police Headquarters. They told Mike Harden, the sergeant on duty, that they were at 'Aunt Emily's Steak and Pizza House' where the incident of Randy Allen Zetterower had occurred. Then, Officer Latham said, "His two daughters were here with him when he passed away." "I heard about that terrible incident just a few minutes ago," said Sergeant Harden. "I am sorry that it happened …especially with his two daughters being there with him at the time that he died." Officer Kostern and I feel the same way," said Officer Latham. Then Officer Latham said, "This brings me to the reason that I called you. Could you arrange to have a woman police officer come to the restaurant and take care of Mr. Randy Zetterower's daughters, Courtney and Celeste, as soon as possible?" Sergeant Harden said, "Let me put you on hold for a moment while I call Officer Beth Coleman and see if she can come now. Sergeant made a call to Officer Coleman, told her about the situation, and asked her if she could go to the restaurant now. Officer Coleman told Sergeant Harden that she could go to the restaurant then and that she was on her way. Sergeant Harden reconnected back to the phone with Officer Latham, and said "I just talked to Officer Coleman, and she will be over there within the next few minutes." "Okay, we appreciate it," said Officer Latham.

When Officer Coleman, the police woman, arrived, at 'Aunt Emily's Steak and Pizza House,' she asked the girls about the name of their 'next of kin.' Courtney acted as the spokesperson for her and Celeste. She told Officer Coleman that their 'next of kin' was Aunt Carol McDora. "Do you have her phone number?" "Yes, I do," said Courtney. "I would also like for you to call a close neighbor that lives down the street from us. Their names are Frank and Sherry Eubanks. I'll give you both phone numbers." Officer Coleman said, "Okay, but let me call your Aunt McDora first." Then, Courtney gave Officer Coleman her Aunt McDora's phone number.

Notes:

Mrs. 'Harris Medical College of New York' husband, Joe Ed McDora had just passed away with prostrate cancer about a year ago. During their marriage of twenty three years, they had no children. Now, after Joe's death, Carol was trying to recover from living alone without her husband or anyone else being with her.

Officer Coleman put Mrs. McDora's phone number into her cell phone and called her. Mrs. McDora said, "Hello." Then Officer Coleman said, "I am Officer Coleman with the Westonia Island Police Department. Is Mrs. McDora there?" "This is she," said Mrs. McDora. Then Officer Coleman began the conversation. "I have some bad news to tell you." Both Carol and Officer Coleman hesitated for a moment without saying a word. Then, Officer Coleman continued, and said, "I do not know if you have heard about what has happened to your brother, Randy, because it may not have had time to be on the TV or radio news; but he just passed away about an hour ago at 'Aunt Emily's Steak and Pizza House.'" With tears in her eyes and pain in her voice, Carol said, "He was my only sibling. Now, he is gone, and I have no one to turn to. I feel like I am all alone in life." Then Officer Coleman quickly spoke up, and said, "You still have Courtney and Celeste. They are here with me now at the restaurant. In just the short time that I have known them, they have stated to me that they love you very much. I want you to come to the restaurant now. Do you think that you can do that?" "Yes, I can. I will be there in about twenty five minutes," said Carol. "After you talk to me, Courtney and Celeste, I would like for you to go home with Courtney and Celeste for a couple of days to keep them company and comfort them." "I'll be happy to do it," said Carol. "I'll see you shortly," said Officer Coleman. "Okay," said Carol. Then both of them said, "Good Bye," and terminated the call.

After Officer Coleman talked to Mrs. Carol McDora on the phone, she got Frank and Sherry's phone number from Courtney and called them. Both of them came over immediately. They were 'in shock' about Randy passing away.

They would never hear his footsteps anymore

Within minutes, Frank and Sherry arrived at the restaurant. They entered the front door and walked over to where Courtney and Celeste were sitting at a table with Officer Coleman. As Courtney and Celeste stood up, Frank and Sherry looked at them, and in unison, said, "We are sorry." Then, each one of them gave a big hug to both Courtney and Celeste.

Both Frank and Sherry sat down at the table and had a conversation with Officer Coleman about what happened with Randy. Of course, there was not too much to tell at that point because no one knew what really happened. During the conversation Mrs. McDora came into the restaurant. She walked over to the table where Courtney, Celeste, and the others were sitting. As everyone at the table looked up at her, Mrs. McDora looked toward Courtney and Celeste, and said, "I am so sorry." There was not enough room for Mrs. McDora to sit with them at the table. So, Frank went over to Betty, who had been Courtney and Celeste's waitress before, and asked her if he could pull another square table next to the one where they were sitting now. Betty said, "Yes, and I will help you move it." After Frank and Betty moved another square table next to the one where the others were sitting, Mrs. McDora sat down. Officer Coleman turned toward Mrs. McDora, and said, "I going to go over some of the same information that I just shared with Frank and Sherry. It will only take about five to ten minutes." "Okay," said Mrs. McDora. Officer Coleman went over everything that she thought that Mrs. McDora needed to know. Then she said, "Mrs. McDora, we talked earlier on the phone about you staying with the girls for at least a couple of days. Are you still willing to take them home and stay with them for a while?" "Yes, I am. In fact, I took time to get some clothes and personal items to bring with me before I came over here." Name turned toward Courtney and Celeste, and said, "Girls are you ready to let Mrs. Mcdora take you home. Remember, we talked about it earlier, and you said that it would be okay. Is this still okay with both of you?" "Yes, it is," said both girls together.

At that point, Frank and Sherry decided that it was time for them to go home. Both of them got up from the tables where everyone was sitting. Just before they turned toward the restaurant door to go home, Frank said, "Courtney and Celeste. We are sorry about your dad. If there is anything that we can do to help you, feel free to call us. I know that you are going to be in good hands with your Aunt Carol McDora." "Thank you," said Courtney. "We appreciate your support in this traumatic experience." "Glad we could help," said Frank. Frank and Sherry walked out the restaurant door and went home.

Courtney, Celeste, and their Aunt McDora went out to their Aunt Carol McDora's car. They all got in her car, and she drove Courtney and Celeste to their home. It was a very bleak moment for Courtney and Celeste. Not a word was spoken by anyone on the way to where Courtney and Celeste lived. It was not because any of three of them had any dissention toward the other one; but there were emotional feelings felt by everyone that could not be expressed. Courtney and Celeste had loss both of their parents. As they entered the door of their home with their Aunt Carol McDora, Courtney and Celeste felt the loneness of their parents not being with them anymore. Of course, there was the possibility of them seeing their mother again, but not their dad. As they thought about the great times that they enjoyed being with him tears came into their eyes. Both of them put their arms around each other and held close for a few moments. Randy, their dad was gone physically, but not in their memory of him being a great and wonderful dad. Aunt Carol knew that they needed to be alone in their thoughts about Randy. So, she said nothing.

Over the next few days, Courtney, Celeste, and their Aunt Carol McDora had some wonderful times together. They were glad to have her with them. It was a comfort just to have someone there. Even so, it still would not be the same without their mother and dad.

The case is under investigation

After an autopsy was performed on Randy, the coroner discovered that he was poisoned. Now, everyone who was in the restaurant at the time Randy was murdered was under suspicion. That is, of course, everyone except Jim, the restaurant manager. According to the waitress, Jim had left before Randy's food was prepared. Also, Emily was not there.

Notes:

The police did not interrogate the restaurant guest shortly after Randy's death earlier because they did not know that Randy had been murdered at that point. Of course, this was going to be a 'lost cause' because anyone at the restaurant including the restaurant patrons could have had a part in the crime.

His funeral

On the day of Randy's funeral, there were many friends and acquaintances that paid their respects to him. It was a very emotional time for everyone …especially Courtney and Celeste. Tears and sad faces were manifested throughout the funeral service.

Fifteen Years Earlier

<u>**From their earlier high school days to when Emily leaves Randy and the girls**</u>

Their Earlier Years Together

Randy and Emily's high school days
Randy met Emily in the tenth grade of high school when they were both <u>fifteen</u>
He dates hers
Later, they met Jim in the same high school at the beginning of the eleventh grade
Emily is <u>strongly</u> attracted to Jim

Randy met Emily, and started dating her in the tenth grade of Fairfield High School in Circleville, Georgia. It seemed that they were really enjoying each other's company on each and every one of their dates. At the end of the tenth grade Randy asked Emily if she would like to go steady with him. She said, "Yes, I would like that very much." Randy told himself that if his relationship with Emily continued going as good in the eleventh and twelfth grade as it had in the tenth grade of high school he planned to ask Emily to marry him after graduation.

Where it all began
The entire story is based on the following paragraph

At the beginning of Randy and Emily's eleventh year in Fairfield High School, both of them went into the 'study hall' one Tuesday afternoon. As they walked through the door they saw a young man whom they had never seen at the high school before. He looked up at them at the same time that they were looking toward him. In a very low, soft tone of voice, Randy said to Emily, "Let's go over and meet him. He must be new here, and it seems that the right thing to do would be to welcome him to Fairfield High School." "Okay," said Emily. That sounds like a good thing to do." Randy and Emily approached the young man. When they got very close to him, he stood up. They all exchanged names. The newcomer's name was Jim Al Benefer. After each one introduced himself/herself, Randy asked Jim, "Are you new to the area?" "Yes I am," said Jim. "My parents and I just moved here from Jamerson, North Carolina." Then Randy said, "It is good to have you with us. I hope you enjoy being here." "Oh, I will," said Jim. Then, as Randy and Emily decided to leave and go over to one of the 'study hall' tables to study, they said, "It is good to meet you, Jim." Jim said, "It is good to meet both of you, too. Have a nice day." Both Randy and Emily said, "You have a good day, Jim." Then Randy and Emily went over to one of the tables in the 'study hall' to study their lessons for the next day at school.

Her feelings change from more than just being a friend
Will it hurt Randy's dreams of him wanting to marry Emily after high school graduation?

Over the next few days after Randy and Emily met Jim, Emily found out that Jim was in her Science class. He had a great personality, and within a couple of weeks, she became attracted to him. During the second month that Emily was around Jim, she wanted to date him. But, over the course of a few more weeks, he never asked her out on a date. It seemed that he just wanted to be friends at that time on a casual friendship basis.

Notes:

During the time that Randy was dating Emily throughout the eleventh and twelfth grade of high school, and on into the time when Randy married her at age eighteen, Emily still had her eyes on Jim. It seemed that her feelings for Jim would always be there.

After Randy graduated from high school, he got a five day week job at 'Bryant's Automotive,' a local automotive service center. Emily went to work at 'Jay's Quick Burger,' a local fast food restaurant.

Randy continued to date Emily after they graduated from Fairfield High School. He thought about marrying her many times over the next few weeks after graduation. Even during their last year of high school, he told himself that he wanted to ask Emily to marry him; but he did not because he felt that they could not financially afford to be together.

On some of Randy and Emily's future dates, Randy gave hints to Emily about wanting to be with her forever. So, she was aware that he would someday soon ask her to marry him. Before the end of two months after graduation, Randy could not wait any longer for them to be together. He took money out of his savings account, went to a jewelry store, and purchased a ring. When Randy and Emily went to dinner the following Saturday night, he got on his knees and proposed to her at the restaurant. He looked into her eyes, and said, "Will you marry me?" She said, "Yes, I'll marry you." The restaurant customers and staff clapped and congratulated them on their forthcoming wedding. After they left the restaurant later, Randy told Emily, "We won't have much initially, but I think we can make it. After all we have each other and that is all we need." Emily did not respond to that comment.

They get married at age <u>eighteen</u>

Just before Randy married Emily, they made the decision to find a nice place to live when they got back from their honeymoon and start their new life together in Westonia Island, New York. They looked throughout the Westonia Island area and saw several small houses and condos that they liked. But, none of them fitted into their budget. At this point, Randy and Emily had to live on a tight budget because Randy was the only one working at this point, and Emily had not decided what she wanted to do. Even the price of the smaller homes that they looked at was more than they could afford. The ones that they could afford were small efficiencies which they did not want over a long term investment of thirty years. If they were going to buy, they needed to have something more than the efficiency ...especially if they had children anytime soon. Both of them had a small savings account at each of their separate banks. Even so, they knew that they could not buy some of the homes that they liked due to their budget restraints. So, they thought about renting an efficiency apartment on a six month lease until they had more time to look at other properties available in the Westonia Island area that they could afford.

The small apartment
Just enough to make ends meet in their new life together
She begins work on her degree in <u>optometry</u>
He helps her pay tuition and fees to go to college

After looking around the Westonia Island area at many of the available apartments that they could rent, Randy and Emily found just the one that they wanted. It was close to where both Randy and Emily worked. Emily had purchased a used car when she went to work at 'Jay's Quick Burger' the fast food place earlier. Randy had purchased a used pickup truck from an employee at 'Bryant's Automotive.' So, both of them had transportation to go to work. In fact, it was only four blocks from where Randy worked. Since neither one of them did not have too far to go to work, the gas money that was saved on the vehicles that they owned helped them on their beginning budget. Of course, there was car and truck insurance that had to be paid; but they managed to take care of it.

Shortly after Randy and Emily returned from their honeymoon, Emily told Randy that she would like to pursue a career in optometry. Randy wanted Emily to have her own unique life and do the things that would make her happy. So, he told her, "It will be great for you to get that degree, and I am going to support you in every way that I can to help you get it." "Thanks," said Emily. The school, 'Harris Medical College of New York,' that she would be going to, was located in Westonia Island, the same city, where they were living in now. This would make it very convenient for her to be close to home while she attended school.

Since Randy was only able to obtain employment as manager at a local automotive service center, his salary was not too good; but with Emily's small income they were able to set up a budget to meet their basic needs. At that point, they sacrificed a lot to make a new life for themselves together. Even though their financial budget was tight, Randy helped Emily pay for her tuition, fees, and books so that she could go to 'Harris Medical College of New York,' and get a degree in optometry. She wanted to have her own business as an Optometrist. During her first year of college, Emily had her work schedule changed to work part time only rather than full time at, 'Jay's Quick Burger,' the fast food restaurant where she had obtained employment shortly after she graduated from high school.

They meet one of their neighbors

Randy and Emily met Frank and Sherry Eubanks at the Westonia island Community Club House at one of the socials that was held each month. The socials were conducted by the Westonia Island community leaders. It was one of the amenities associated with being a resident of the Westonia island community. These community leaders were elected each year by the residents. Frank and Sherry lived about two blocks from Randy and Emily in the same neighborhood.

Even though Emily is married, she <u>continually</u> keeps in <u>touch</u> with him

Emily still had Jim's phone number from high school. Rather than have him call her, she calls him so that no one, except Sherry Eubanks, would know that she is maintaining contact with him.

Government support for school
Their <u>first child</u> at age <u>nineteen</u>
Looking for another place to live

After Emily's first year in college, she was able to obtain financial help from a government grant for her school tuition, fees, books, and living expenses. She was able to quit work completely and focus all of her attention on her studies. The extra money that was now available for living expenses helped them to have some extra spending money and even open up a savings account at their local bank.

In less than a year after Randy and Emily moved into the small apartment when they were eighteen, Emily became pregnant. During April of the following year, she had a girl that they named Courtney. Within a few months after Courtney was born, Randy and Emily made a serious effort to look for something that had more room than the small apartment that they were in now. The extra money that was available for Emily's living expenses from the government grant that she had been receiving starting with her second year in college would be enough to help them get something better than their small apartment.

The condo

After checking out houses and condos in the area, they found a condominium close to the Westonia Island beach of the Atlantic Ocean. It was in Blue Surf Estates in Westonia Island, New York. The builder and community developer had a special promotion so that purchasers for a short time could get a condo with ten percent down and only nine hundred and eighty five dollars closing costs. The payments on a thirty year mortgage were reasonable, too.

She meets a man who was studying 'internal medicine' to be a family doctor

While Emily was working on her degree in optometry, she met Mr. Andy Edwin King who was studying to be a medical doctor. He told her that he was going to set up his practice as a 'Family Medical Doctor' in 'Internal Medicine' in Westonia Island, New York where she and Randy lived.

He becomes their family doctor

Doctor Andy Edwin King graduates from 'Harris Medical College of New York' within a few months after Emily meets him. Later, Doctor Andy Edwin King whom Emily met while attending 'Harris Medical College of New York,' becomes their family doctor. She tells Randy that Doctor Andy Edwin King was in the same medical college that she went to, and it would be good to have him as their family doctor. Randy welcomes the suggestion, and says, "Okay, Emily. Let's see how we like him."

Their second child is born

One and one half years after Courtney is born, Emily becomes pregnant again in October. On the following year at Randy and Emily's age of twenty one, Emily has the baby during the latter part of June. It is another girl. They named her Celeste. Doctor King helped Emily with the birth of Celeste. Courtney was two years old in April of the year that Celeste was born.

They become close friends during that time

For the past four years that Randy and Emily had been married from age eighteen to age twenty two, Emily and Sherry had become very close friends. During that same time frame, Randy and Frank's friendship was totally different. It was strictly on a casual acquaintances basis only. Due to Emily and Sherry's close relationship, Emily shared a lot of her personal life and her everyday life affairs with Sherry …probably more than she did with Randy.

She graduates at age twenty five

At this point, Emily has completed three years of the five years required for her to get an optometry degree. Now, after Celeste is born, she completes the final two years of her education and graduates with the Optometry Degree. She gets her optometry license and her business license to start her business as an optometris. Then, she rents office space and sets up her own practice as an optometrist in Westonia Island, New York where she and Randy lived. From the very beginning of her business venture, Emily proved to be a good optometrist. Not only was she a good optometrist, but she was also a great business person as well. Within just a few months, she had a very successful business in the field of optometry.

Randy was pleased that Emily was doing well in her business. But, at times, it seemed to bother him. Due to her over one hundred thousand dollars a year income as compared to his small salary of thirty three thousand dollars a year, it made him feel that she was the 'bread-winner' in the family. Even though it bothered him, he was still able to, most of the time when these thoughts went through his mind, dismissed them so that it would not hurt his marriage by him being jealous of her salary. He made up his mind that he was going to think thoughts of the good income that both of them had together rather than thoughts of: "She makes more than me, and therefore appears to be the 'bread-winner' in the family."

Notes:

Since Randy only worked weekdays, he had weekends off to be with his wife, Emily, their two daughters, Courtney Anne, and Celeste Jane. At times, he would do extra work to help friends on Saturday, but not too often since that was time to be spent with his wife and daughters.

Larry V. Johnson

She Still Cares For Him

Her feelings for Jim are still there
She still keeps in touch with him
His earlier childhood and teenage problems were carried over into adulthood

Even though Randy had now married Emily, she still had feelings for Jim that surfaced often. Those feelings created a desire in her to keep in contact with Jim as a very close friend.

Throughout Jim's childhood and his earlier school years, he had been a 'trouble maker' and a bully. During the last two years while he was in Fairfield High School, it seemed that he had turned his life around and was going to be a good citizen in society. After graduating from Fairfield High School, Jim got a good job with a local bank in Westonia Island, New York where he, Randy, and Emily lived.

Throughout all of the years that Emily was married to Randy, she kept 'close ties' with Jim. She never saw Jim; but she called him often and stayed 'in touch' with him. No one knew about the 'close ties' that Emily kept with Jim except Frank's wife, Sherry Eubanks.

She buys a Thunderbird for herself
She buys him a 'top-of-the-line' Harley Davidson Motorcycle

Emily bought a Thunderbird for herself, and even though she still cared about Jim, she bought Randy a motorcycle. After all, she needed to let everyone think that she cared for Randy and no one else …which of course was false since her feelings were strongly for Jim.

The restaurant
Randy and Emily are now <u>twenty eight</u>
Courtney is <u>nine</u>: Born when Randy and Emily were <u>nineteen</u>
Celeste is <u>seven</u>: Born when Randy and Emily were <u>twenty one</u>

At age twenty eight, Emily has made enough money to discontinue her optometry business and buy a restaurant. This was the second one of her dreams when she was a teenager that she hoped someday to fulfill. Everyone told her that she seemed to know a lot about food and the different ways to make excellent meals along with delicious desserts. Most of them suggested that she become a gourmet cook. Now that dream had come true. She named the restaurant 'Aunt Emily's Steak and Pizza House.'

Shortly after Emily opened her restaurant, she became known as a person who would be doing well in society in general, and she developed a good reputation with everyone. She served delicious southern home-cooked meals and desserts. Restaurant guest came from hundreds of miles away just to taste her good food and exquisite desserts.

He Is Incarcerated

He is incarcerated at age <u>twenty nine</u>
Emily is the <u>same age</u> at this point

When Jim Al Benefer turned twenty nine, something happened in his life that caused him to embezzle funds from the bank where he worked. In addition, he was incarcerated for passing off bad checks and stealing identities from several wealthy clients who patronized the bank where he worked. After being convicted of the crime, he was incarcerated for three years.

Eleven years later after graduating from Fairfield High School at age eighteen, they are <u>twenty nine</u> years old
She has now known him for <u>fourteen</u> years ...from age <u>sixteen</u> <u>in the eleventh grade</u> to age <u>twenty nine</u> now
He is released from prison

Celeste's mother, Emily, had now rekindled her love very strongly again for Jim Al Benefer who had just got out of prison about three weeks ago. Both of them were now thirty two years old. Unknowingly to her husband, Randy, she had been keeping in contact with Jim for the three years while he was in prison plus the time since she, Randy, and Jim had graduated from Fairfield high school. Throughout those years from the eleventh grade in Fairfield High School to the time Jim was released from prison, Emily kept in contact with Jim. She called him at least twice a week.

He has a 'change of heart' ...or does he?

Now things apparently had changed and Jim let Emily know that he had fallen in love with her ...at least that is what he told her when she went to visit him while he was in prison. His romantic sayings and actions when she visited him deeply rekindled the affectionate feelings that she had for him when they were in Fairfield High School. Her feelings that she had for Jim were rekindled when he said, "I love you." each time that she went to the prison to see him during the three years that he was there.

At this point, the story continues from the time that Randy became ill in Emily's restaurant earlier and was pronounced dead. The following starts after Randy's funeral

Larry V. Johnson

Their Life Goes On

Her marriage to Jim after Randy is murdered
She develops a bad health condition
Does her bad health affect her life?

Within a couple of days after Randy's death, Jim proposed to Emily, she accepted, and they got married. Many of Emily's closest friends were shocked that she married Jim almost immediately after Randy's death; but they did not say anything about it.

Shortly after Emily married Jim she started having health problems. At times she felt physically weak. The condition started when she was married to Randy. The condition was not too severe, but it was bad enough that she could <u>not</u> take care of another person if she had, too. Jim knew about her health problem, and was very supportive and took care of her when she needed help with the condition. Emily wanted to get custody of Celeste; but Doctor King, whom she met in medical school and was still her family doctor, told the County Superior Court officials that it would not be wise because of Emily's health condition.

Notes:

It appeared that Jim loved Emily initially just before he got out of prison. But, the love that he said he had for her may not have been true love <u>since it only lasted a short time</u>. He only pretended to love her; and later after she married him, she discovered it. She was his meal-ticket and help since he had been in prison. He may have had a difficult time finding a job if she had not helped him by '<u>taking him in</u>.'

She came to take care of Courtney and Celeste at age <u>twenty eight</u>
The police still have no leads or clues concerning Randy's death
Courtney is <u>thirteen</u>
Celeste is <u>eleven</u>

After Randy was poisoned at the young age of thirty two, his sister, Carol McDora, came to live with Celeste and Courtney in their home so that she could take care of them. She was twenty eight at the time. Both Courtney and Celeste were able to live with their Aunt Carol without any problems.

At this point, the police had no clues or leads as to who murdered Randy. They had no suspects in or out of their custody and no motivation as to why someone would want to kill him. Even without any evidence or leads, the case was still under investigation.

Global warming affected them

Global warming temperatures caused the oceans and other bodies of water throughout the world to rise. This was due to the glaciers in the northern hemisphere melting. The Atlantic Ocean began slowly to cover the beach area in front of Carol McDora, Courtney, and Celeste's condo. Over a few days, the water came up to the condo. They were warned by the Westonia Island Emergency Management Center (EMC) to vacate the condo. Aunt Carol suggested that they move into 'Joe's Stay All Week Motel' for a few days until they could decide what they need to do about finding another place to live. Just as Carol, Courtney, and Celeste were getting some personal items and other things that that may need to make life easy for them while living temporarily in the motel, water started coming into the front door of the Condo. Celeste did not have flood insurance or the money to purchase it. Of course, it was too late to think about why she did not purchase it now. The water coming from the ocean was happening now and starting to damage the condo. They waded in water as they walked from the condo to Aunt Carol McDora's car and drove in the direction away from the Kingleton Public Beach area.

Carol McDora, Courtney, and Celeste lose their home in the beach area

The Global Warming phenomenon had caused the water in the oceans to rise to the point that Carol McDora, Celeste and her sister, Courtney lose their condo because the water damages it too much to live in.

Uncle Cecil Jase Zetterower

Celeste had an uncle whom she admired. His name was Cecil Jase Zetterower. He also liked her very much. He had health problems that caused him to pass away when he was in his late seventies.

His will was disclosed
<u>Location of the property</u> that she inherited
Giving her property a name

Celeste's Uncle Cecil left her and Courtney thirty acres of beautiful land and the condo that was on it in his will. This condo was back far enough from the beach area so that the rising waters did not affect it. The condo and land that Uncle Cecil left them was available at just the right time when they lost the condo that they were in due to the problems of rising waters in the Atlantic Ocean which caused by the effects of 'Global Warming.' According to his will, Uncle Cecil gave Courtney and Celeste his condo because he felt bad about Courtney and Celeste losing Emily, their mother, Randy, their dad, and he knew that they needed another place to stay after losing their condo on the beach.

The condo that Celeste had inherited from her Uncle Cecil was on thirty acres of land in the Westonia Island Sound area. Initially, Celeste thought that she had inherited Uncle Cecil's condo and only one or two acres of land. When the trustee had read the will, it only stated that she had inherited the condo along with the land that it was on. When she and Carol McDora went to the Morganton Courthouse, they found out that it was not the one or two acres that Celeste thought that it would be; but the condo was on thirty acres. Celeste knew that there were many acres of land around the condo; but she did not realize that it went with her condo and land inheritance. Celeste, Courtney Anne, and Carol McDora enjoyed staying in the condo that Celeste's Uncle Cecil had left.

Shortly after Courtney, Celeste and Carol McDora moved into the condo on the thirty acre property that Uncle Cecil had left Celeste in his will, Celeste thought about giving the beautiful thirty acre property and condo a name. After thinking about several names that would be appropriate for it, she finally decided on the name Danielle's Vineyard. Over eight hundred feet on the front side of the property faced the six mile long 'Kingleton Public Beach.' This beach was within one thousand feet of the front of the condo.

Its location in regard to the beach and adjacent properties

Danielle's Vineyard was physically located on the upper northern section of the Kingleton Public Beach area. It was bordered on the northern side by 'The Rock'. 'The Rock' was a three thousand foot section of the six mile 'Kingleton Public Beach.' In that area were rock formations on an eight to twenty foot high hill area. Immediately north of 'The Rock' was a light house owned by the Federal Government. On the other side of Danielle's Vineyard was the historic and world famous 'Westonia Island Sound' property of Jan and Sylvia's 'Ocean Crest' Villas. It was a four hundred and fifty room hotel located right at the beach.

There was more
The additional inheritance

Uncle Cecil Zetterower also left Courtney and Celeste $20,000 each that had to be cashed in from an insurance policy that he left.

In addition, Celeste's Uncle Cecil also had a cabin cruiser. He had it stored in a marina boat storage area in an inlet just off the Atlantic Ocean. It was close to where Celeste lived now. In addition to the condo, the land, and the money, that Uncle Cecil gave Celeste in his will, it also specified that she was to get the cabin cruiser, too.

Celeste's obsession

Carol McDora, Courtney, and Celeste continued enjoying their daily life in the new condo. One of their main inside activities was watching TV together. Both Carol McDora and Courtney could not help but notice that Celeste liked to watch crime scene shows and the solving of them more than any other TV program or show. Some of her best TV programs were those pertaining to criminal cases.

Throughout her younger years, Celeste developed a passion for wanting to have a career in 'Criminal Justice.' She continually told Carol McDora and Courtney that she wanted to help solve her dad's murder.

Their Emotional Problems

Her Emotional Breakdown

It affected her life
Placed in a rehabilitation unit of the New York State Rehabilitation Service Center
Courtney was eleven at the time
Celeste was nine at the time
Jim and Emily are thirty three

Courtney Anne cannot deal with Emily and Randy not being with them anymore. She missed Emily and her dad to the point that she became emotionally unstable at age eleven. It caused her to have an emotional breakdown. Their Aunt Carol McDora, who was still taking care of them in their home talked to the Department of Family and Children's Services (DFAC) about her problem. They suggested that Courtney be placed in the New York State Rehabilitation Service Center which was about fifty three miles from where they lived. Reluctantly, Courtney went there. But, it was only because she knew that it would help her get better. Carol McDora and Celeste visited her every week.

She is back home at age <u>twelve</u>

One year after Courtney was in the New York State Rehabilitation Service Center on the day before her twelfth birthday Celeste asked her Aunt Carol McDora to try and get Courtney Anne to come back and live with them. Carol reminded Celeste that she would have to check on how Courtney was doing. If she had proven to be emotionally stable, then there could be a possibility that she would be able to return home. Then Carol said, "Let's go get a birthday present for Courtney so that we can take it to her tomorrow." As they walked out the door, Carol did some thinking, and said, "On second thought, let's go by the New York State Rehabilitation Service Center and ask them if Courtney can be released on her birthday tomorrow." "Do you really mean it?" said Celeste. "Yes, I definitely do," said Carol.

Carol and Celeste went immediately over to the New York State Rehabilitation Service Center to talk to the director, Mrs. Monica Grizzle, to see if Courtney could come home tomorrow on her birthday. On the way over Carol remembered that Mrs. Grizzle at the Center had told her about a week ago that there could be a possibility Courtney could complete the program and return home in the next few days. Tomorrow would be within the few days that the director had made that statement. So, Courtney's release and returning home could happen on her birthday.

When Carol talked to the director Mrs. Grizzle at the New York State Rehabilitation Service Center, Mrs. Grizzle said, "I was just getting ready to call you. I feel that Courtney is ready to go back home to be with you and Celeste. She has improved to the point that she can even make that decision on her own if she wants to."

Notes:

Courtney Anne came back to live with Celeste after being placed in a Rehabilitation Program for one year. She had been placed there at age eleven because of her 'emotional breakdown' which appeared to be a result of her mother, Emily, leaving the family and her dad, Randy, dying from being poisoned.

Celeste was ten at the time that Courtney Anne came back to live with her in the condo that their Uncle Cecil had given them earlier in his will. Courtney Anne was twelve at that time.

Courtney Anne lived with her Aunt Carol McDora and Celeste for nine years from age twelve to age twenty one. This was the same time that Celeste at age nineteen met Scotty when he was twenty one.

Emily And The Emotionally Disturbing Time Of her Life

Notes:

During this time of Emily's life, she was beginning to have emotional distress. The emotional distress problem was in addition to the problem that she had of becoming physically weak at times. Both of Emily's problems together affected her everyday life in a very big and dramatic way.

Larry V. Johnson

The Second And Third Murder

Jim, Emily's second husband, knew too much
He <u>becomes ill</u> during one of his meals

<u>Notes</u>:

One month after Jim married Emily, he made an appointment to go see Doctor Andy Edwin King at 10 A.M. on a Monday about a sore throat problem. This doctor was the same one that Randy, Emily, and their two daughters went to before Randy was murdered and Emily married Jim.

On the day of his appointment, Jim walked into Doctor King's Office and went up to the receptionist window to check in. When Randy came up to the receptionist's window, he looked at Susan Simmons, the receptionists, and said, "In addition to my exam today, I have some very important information that I may share with Doctor King about Randy's murder." "Okay," said Susan.

Susan knew the murderer. So, she called him/her on her cell phone while Jim was in one of the exam rooms, and told him/her that Jim had probably told Doctor King that he/she murdered Randy. The murderer said, "I need to take quick action now to get rid of Jim before he can testify against me.

While Susan was talking to the murderer on her cell phone, Doctor King examined Jim, gave him a prescription, and told him to come back to his office in three days on the following Thursday. Then Doctor King said to Jim, "We can see then could see if your sore throat is getting better. Jim left the office and went home.

On Thursday morning Jim went to his managerial job at 5:00 A.M. at Emily's restaurant like he always did five days a week. Jim took a fifteen minute break after working two hours. Then he worked until Emily came in at 9:22 A.M. so that she could take over when Jim left for his appointment to go see Doctor King. She was supposed to have been there at 9:00 A.M. But, since she was late, Jim knew that if he ate a complete meal like he usually did, he would be late for his doctor's appointment. So, he got a sandwich, a glass of sweet Tea, and sat down at one of the tables close to the kitchen entrance.

Notes:

The kitchen entrance and exit door was used by waitresses who were taking food and drink orders to the restaurant customers.

Just as Jim took his first bite of his sandwich, he felt nauseated. He quickly drank some of his sweet Tea. That did not help. Within seconds he begins to feel like throwing up. He gets up from his chair and rushes toward the men's room. As he was leaving his table to go to the men's restroom which was located close to the restaurant entrance, Lori, one of the waitresses came out of the kitchen door next to his table and stepped in front of him. She was taking an order of food and drinks on a tray to four customers at a table about ten feet from where Jim had been sitting. In his haste to get to the men's room, Jim knocked her over and she fell to the floor. The food and drinks went everywhere. It got on several customers at nearby tables as well as on the four customers that she was taking the food to. When Lori fell to the floor, Jim threw up on the floor next to her. Then his body fell on top of her torso area as he died. Lori, not knowing that Jim was dead, tried to get up. But, Jim was too heavy and she could not move. Lori screamed for Jim to get off of her. Betty was there in the restaurant at the time. Just as she had done for Randy when he died, she picked up the phone next to the cash register, and called 911. At the same time that Betty was making the call, two men in the restaurant came over and pulled Jim off of Lori. At that point, Lori knew that Jim was out; so she, along with the others in the restaurant waited for the Para Medics to see if they could revive him. None of them knew that he was dead at that point. The Para Medics were there within minutes. Betty recognized the two Para Medics as the same ones who came to the restaurant when she called them for Randy. After examining Jim, one of the two Para Medics said, "We won't be able to revive him. He's dead." When they stated that Jim was dead, Lori the waitress that he had fallen on passed out. She was in shock from having a dead man on her. After recovering from the shock, she felt very unclean and had to go home to get a shower.

During the entire ordeal, some of the customers left the restaurant; one or two of those who left were probably 'in-a-state-of-panic and did not pay for their meal. Due to the situation, no one said anything as they walked out the door without paying.

She becomes involved with <u>another man</u>
His gift to her

Emily met Jesse Lee Wilbanks, another man, who came into the restaurant often. After they buried her second husband Jim, Emily goes out with Jesse who was very wealthy. Jesse sets her up with a chain of restaurants world-wide that has the same name of 'Aunt Emily's Steak and Pizza House' that she started two years ago in Morganton, New York.

Doctor King's Dilemma

Notes:

Doctor King found out from Jim Al Benefer, when Jim came into Doctor King's office for a sore throat problem, who murdered Randy Zetterower. After Jim revealed that information to Doctor King, Jim was murdered. Immediately after Jim was murdered, Doctor King typed several notes on his computer saying that whoever opened the envelope with the notes in it would have to go to his wife, Mary, to get a locked box that had another envelope in it with the murderer's name on it. He printed out the notes, put them in an envelope, and gave them to his wife, Mary. He told her, "Give this envelope to Doctor Lancaster if anything happens to me. I have a paper in an envelope that has the murderer's name on it in a locked box. I am giving you the locked box and the key. Again, if anything happens to me, do not give anyone the box except the District Attorney at the trial of the murders ...if there is one." "Okay," said Mary. "But I hope nothing happens to you."

Now Doctor King knew that he could be the next victim since Jim told him who murdered Randy. In fact, the same person who murdered Randy may have murdered Jim. The murderer discovered from Susan, Doctor King's secretary, that Doctor King knew who murdered Randy and Jim.

They attended the restaurant often
He becomes ill on this visit to the restaurant

Doctor King and his wife, Mary, enjoyed going to 'Emily's Steak and Pizza House' for breakfast. They usually went about once a month. Early on a Saturday morning, two weeks after Jim was murdered, Doctor King told Mary, "We have not been to Emily's restaurant in a while. Would you like to go to the restaurant for breakfast?" "That sounds like a good idea. I'd love, too." Both of them got ready and went to the restaurant.

Betty, one of the waitresses, took their order. Doctor King ordered two eggs scrambled well, sausage, hash browns, a biscuit, and 'regular' coffee. Mary ordered the same thing.

After Betty took their order, she brought Doctor King and Mary their coffee, and said, "Your order will be ready in a few minutes." After Doctor King and Mary engaged themselves in some small talk, Betty came to their table with each ones breakfast on a large tray. She placed Mary's breakfast in front of her on the table. Then, she put Doctor King's breakfast in front of him.

Doctor King liked the eggs and the way they were cooked at Emily's restaurant. He looked at them and decided to eat them first. After two bites of the eggs, he felt like throwing up, and he became deathly sick. He quickly placed his fork on the edge of his plate and picked up his coffee cup. Just before he could get even a sip of coffee, his head went forward toward his plate with the hot coffee spilling all over him and everywhere else. The hot coffee was burning his body, and he screamed. Then, as Doctor King's head fell over into his breakfast plate the fork that he was using to eat his eggs with flipped over and pierced his right eye ball. He screamed again just as he was dying and blood flowed from the eye ball just as he fell to the floor on the right side of his chair. Mary looked on in horror. She got up and looked over at her husband. The restaurant patrons screamed and many of them left the restaurant as police ...and, yes, the same paramedics that took care of Randy and Jim earlier came to this death scene. They wanted to be professional in the handling of Doctor King's death by not comparing this one to Randy and Jim's death; but they could not believe a third death had happened in the same restaurant in just less than two years. They knew that it could have been a murder just like the ones that happened with

Randy and Jim; but they could not make that judgment decision or even talk about it. When Mary found out that her husband was dead, and probably murdered, she told herself that whoever murdered Randy and Jim murdered her husband, Doctor King. She left the restaurant feeling lonely and hurt about what had happened.

They have no leads

The law enforcement officials in the City of <u>Moganton</u>, New York still had no idea as to who could have committed the crimes. There were no leads or clues as to who could have poisoned Emily's two previous husbands and the doctor. They had the New York Crime Lab to check the food in the kitchen area thoroughly. Everything was being done properly and in order with the way the food was stored in the refrigerator, in the freezer, and the way it was prepared and cooked. The restaurant got a score of one hundred percent in everything that was done in the kitchen area as well as how clean it was. Nothing could be found wrong with anything in the restaurant.

It's a '<u>cold case</u>'
Courtney is <u>fourteen</u>
Celeste is <u>twelve</u>

No one could solve the case involving the three murders at Emily's restaurant. After two years when Courtney turned fourteen and Celeste turned twelve, the case was regarded as a 'cold case.'

Section Two

Celeste and The Tall Stranger At 'The Rock'

Seven Years Later

<u>Celeste</u> is now <u>nineteen</u>
She makes the decision to become an attorney
She enters <u>Royalton Agnes College</u> and pursues a degree
in 'Criminal Justice'
Vows to find her dad's murderer
<u>Courtney</u> is now <u>twenty one</u>
She also enters <u>Royalton Agnes College</u> to pursue a
degree in 'Community Counseling'

Celeste entered Royalton Agnes College to study to be an attorney at age nineteen. Then after getting the (**Name of degree for attorneys**) degree she takes and passes the bar exam.

When Celeste entered college, she was determined that she would find out who murdered her dad. She vowed that justice would be done when she found the person ...regardless of who they were.

Courtney entered Royalton Agnes College to pursue a degree in 'Community Counseling.' Now, both sisters were going to the same college.

Introducing Scotty John Williams

His wife's problem
He comes up to 'Westonia Island Sound'
Janelle's Vineyard
'The Rocks' part of the beach area

It was now 6:20 A.M. on a Tuesday morning in the month of July in Westbay, New Jersey. The temperature was a warm sixty nine degrees. Scotty John Williams and his wife, Julie Lynn Williams, were sleeping soundly on their king size bed. At exactly 6:30 A.M. the alarm woke them up. Both of them got out of bed, went to separate bathrooms to get showers, dressed, and went out the door of their home to have breakfast at 'New Beach Restaurant' ...a local restaurant in the area. Julie Lynn had been having pains in her chest area and in her left breast. They had an appointment with Dr. Doctor Susan Keller at 9 A.M. that morning. Scotty wanted to accompany Julie Lynn to Doctor Susan Keller's office that morning. He wanted to know, just like Julie did, about what was going on in her chest area. Both Scotty and Julie had taken off from their respective jobs on a day of sick leave.

After Scotty and Julie ate breakfast, Scotty drove them to Doctor Susan Keller's office. Julie was taken by Charlotte, Dr. Keller's nurse, to one of the examination rooms. When Dr. Keller came in and examined Julie, she discovered a lump in Julie's left breast. It had become very large at that point. Dr. Keller told Scotty and Julie that Julie needed to see Doctor Richard Harrison, a specialist, immediately. He asked his secretary to call Doctor Harrison at the 'Doctor's Medical

Center' which was located adjacent to the Westbay, New Jersey Hospital. The secretary was able to set up an appointment for Julie to see Doctor Harrison that afternoon. Upon examining her, Doctor Harrison said that they needed to start 'chemo treatments' within the next two days.

Julie went through the rugged turmoil of the 'chemo treatments' for five months; but it was to no avail. The cancer had already spread to her chest area and was now rapidly going throughout her body. Everything was done to keep her from feeling the pain of the cancer that was destroying her body. Scotty was very upset to see Julie Lynn going through so much pain and turmoil. It especially hurt him when he could not do anything to help her.

Within six months of the time that Julie Lynn began chemo treatments, she passed away. She had waited too long before taking her yearly mammogram checkups this time. Relatives and friends mourned the loss of a wonderful woman.

For a while, Scotty had problems realizing that Julie Lynn was not with him anymore. The sadness and grief associated with the loss, made it difficult for him to go back to work at his job with The New Jersey Electric Power Company (NJE). Scotty's manager, Joe Hazelton, at NJE told Scotty that he could take some time off before he came back to work. Even before Joe told him about taking time off, Scotty had already decided to do it. His benefits package provided for a week off for grievance with pay. Within a week, he came back to work with NJE. He had now been with them for three years. Scotty knew that it would be a consolation for him to work as much as he could so that he could keep his mind off of how much he missed Julie Lynn.

Several weeks after Julie Lynn's funeral, Scotty thought that he could make it without finding another woman in his life. He just knew that no one could ever replace Julie Lynn. But, as the days turned into weeks, and the weeks turned into months, he became very lonely. One of his friends at work told him about 'The Dating Connection' on the internet, and told him that he may want to check it out.

One evening Scotty got on the internet and went to 'The dating Connection' Web Site. After signing in and paying a fee, he looked over the women that were within his age range of twenty five. He saw many women from age twenty to thirty two that he liked. Of all of the women that he saw, he became interested in Jennifer Anne Jones more than all of the others. She lived in the Westonia Island Sound area of New York. Scotty made a connection with Jennifer through 'The Dating Connection' Web Site and got her cell phone number.

Over the next few days after Scotty got Jennifer's cell phone number, he called her two times. On each call, they shared things about each other and had an enjoyable conversation. After talking to Jennifer for a few minutes on the second call, Scotty asked Jennifer, "Jennifer, would it be possible for me to come up to visit you this coming weekend?" Jennifer knew that Scotty was interested in her, and she was interested in him. So, she said, "Let me check my calendar." After a few seconds of silence, Jennifer responded, "Usually, I have something planned almost every weekend. But, next weekend looks okay." "Great," said Scotty. "I am looking forward to it." "I am too," said Jennifer. "Can you give me your address?" Jennifer told Scotty where she lived. It was in a condo that she rented next to Jan and Sylvia's 'Ocean Crest' Villas.

After Scotty and Jennifer completed their call, Scotty went on-line on the internet immediately and checked out the hotels in the Westonia Island Sound area. After looking at the accommodations and rates of several hotels, he saw exactly the one where he wanted to stay. It was the 'White Surf Ocean Front Hotel.' They had ocean front rooms, and they had a special that weekend. If he made reservations and stayed both

Friday and Saturday nights, he would get a full free breakfast on Saturday and Sunday morning. Scotty wasted no time in calling the number on their Web Site, and made reservations with a credit card for the following week end.

On the following Friday night, Scotty arrived at the 'White Surf Ocean Front Hotel.' After checking into the hotel and going to his room, he called Jennifer, and they set up a dinner date at 'Ocean House Restaurant' for that evening.

Scotty and Jennifer appeared to have a wonderful evening together on that Friday night at the restaurant; but things did not seem to be going as smoothly as it should have between them. Both of them felt like 'distant cousins,' and they could not even begin to develop a good rapport with each other. The chemistry was just not there between them. Scotty told himself that it was probably because they had just met, and they would have to get to knowing each other more. Then he told himself that after he and Jennifer spent more time together it would help their relationship. So, just before Scotty and Jennifer finished eating, Scotty asked Jennifer, "Would you like to go for an early 7 A.M. walk on the beach with me tomorrow morning?" "I'd like that," said Jennifer.

Notes:

Jennifer felt the same way that Scotty did that Friday evening; but she was trying to make the best of it. She knew that Scotty had spent money and taken time to come up to be with her, and she did not want to hurt his feelings by saying that she did not want to be with him anymore ...at least not at that point.

After their Friday night date, Scotty went to 'The Rock' on 'Kingleton Public Beach.' He went up to the top of the twenty foot high hilly terrain and rock formation area of 'The Rock' and sat on one of the huge rocks overlooking the beach below. He looked behind him at the light house which was about two hundred feet away in a north western direction. As the light within the light house rotated it cast intermittent beams of light continually throughout the area.

Scotty looked at his watch. It was about 11:55 P.M. He had gone to the area because it seemed to be a quiet place for him to do some serious thinking about his relationship with Jennifer.

The geographical layout of the area as <u>also</u> described earlier

About three thousand feet of the six mile 'Kingleton Public Beach' was adjacent to a twenty foot high hilly terrain area with rock formations. It was physically located on the upper northern section of the six mile beach area. This hilly terrain area was part of 'The Rock' in the 'Kingleton Public Beach' area on Westonia Island Sound. 'The Rock' area had beautiful rock formations that were developed by the wind and the high tide from the Atlantic Ocean. Janelle's Vineyard that Celeste owns was adjacent to the north side of 'The Rock.' 'The Rock' was where Scotty saw Celeste the first time. Within two hundred feet of 'The Rock' was a light house owned by the Federal government.

She Appears

For several minutes Scotty tried to think of a way to handle the situation between him and Jennifer. At one point shortly after midnight, Scotty began looking out over the area below him. He continued thinking about what he was going to say to Jennifer on the next morning about breaking up with her. Suddenly his thoughts were interrupted by someone walking on the beach below. The intermittent rotating light from the light house behind Scotty intermittently cast enough beams of light so that he could see that the person was a woman. She was strolling toward the northern part of the beach at a steady pace with a huge Greyhound Dog.

Initially, when Scotty first saw the woman, he could not see her too well. When the woman and the dog got close to where Scotty was sitting on the big rock on the twenty foot high rock wall formation, her dog stopped and directed his attention toward Scotty. Then he started to bark. As the woman and her dog came within two feet of the twenty foot high rock wall that Scotty was on, she looked in his direction ...probably to see what was causing her dog to bark. As the woman looked up at Scotty's location, he was not there because he had moved quickly behind some rocks adjacent to where he was sitting. Just before Scotty moved behind the rocks, he was able to see the woman's facial features very plainly and clearly in the bright moon light. She was beautiful and had long wavy hair that was blowing in the winds from the ocean below. Her dog stopped barking, and the woman walked away with her dog in the northern direction of the beach. Shortly after the woman left the area, Scotty thought to himself that some women would not have dared to go out by themselves after dark anywhere on the beach. So, why she was out at that time of night by herself?

Notes:

Scotty could tell that the woman was very bold and brave because she did not run away in a hurry when her dog started barking. She looked in the direction that her dog was facing when he barked. After he stopped barking, she walked casually away without any thought of the danger that could have been there.

Usually Celeste would go for a walk on the beach twice a day while it was daylight; but today, on a Friday, she decided to go at mid-night with her very large Greyhound dog, George III. She missed her dad and needed some quiet time to herself. So, even though she usually went in the day time, she decided to take today's walk at mid-night on the beach.

He breaks up with Jennifer because he sees no future with her

When Scotty saw Jennifer the next morning on Saturday, he said, "Rather than go for a walk on the beach now like we had planned, can we have breakfast at 'White Surf Ocean Front Hotel' Restaurant? There is something that I need to talk to you about." "Okay," said Jennifer. After looking at the menu and placing their order with the waitress, Scotty looked at Jennifer, and said, "I went to 'The Rocks' area on the northern section of the beach last night after we had dinner together. While there, I did some thinking about you and me. I really do not know how to say this except to tell you like it is in regard to our relationship. At that point, the waitress came with their breakfast and drinks. It seemed that Scotty was having difficulty telling Jennifer how he felt about her. On the Friday night before, Jennifer felt that things were not going too good, and she had the same feelings that Scotty had about their relationship. Therefore, she knew what Scotty was going to say. So, she said, "I think I know how you feel. So, let me help out. I have also been doing some thinking, and I feel that we can only be friends and nothing more. Is that how you feel?" "Yes, it is," said Scotty. "I hope you do not feel bad about it." "No, I do not," said Jennifer. I think that our breakfast has gotten cold. Just before Jenifer made that comment, the waitress brought Scotty the check for their breakfast. Jennifer momentarily looked at Scotty. Then, she said, "Excuse me. I need to go." Jennifer got up from her chair at the table and turns toward the restaurant door to leave. Scotty quickly puts the amount of money for the check plus the tip on the table and follows Jennifer to her car. Before Jennifer got into her car, Scotty said, "Can we still be friends?" "Yes," said Jennifer. Then both of them went their separate ways.

Notes:

On the next morning which was Saturday, Scotty and Jennifer, at Scotty's request and suggestion, went to the hotel restaurant for breakfast rather than walk together on the beach that they had planned to do earlier. Before he could get the exact words out to tell Jennifer that he does not have feelings for her, she knows what he is going to say and lets him know in a nice way that she feels the same way and has no feelings for him either. They tell each other that they will still be friends only and nothing more.

Scotty called his manager, Joe Hazleton, at home and told him that he would like to stay one more day at Westonia Island Sound, which was going to be the following Monday, and use a day of vacation for that day. He was hoping that he could within that two day period of Sunday and Monday see the beautiful woman that he saw last Saturday night walking again on the beach. He knew that there was more than a possibility that she was married. But, he wanted to find out. There was something 'in the air' about why he wanted to meet her. He did not know why. But, he knew that he wanted to talk to her.

At about 11:15 P.M., Scotty went to the same location that he was at on the Friday night before. He waited from 11:30 P.M. to 12:45 A.M.; but the woman never showed up. He went back to his hotel room and thought about taking a nap since it was close to the next day. But, his deep thoughts about wanting to see the woman again caused him to not be able to go to sleep. So, he watched TV from 1 A.M. to 6 A.M. Even though he could not sleep, he 'dozed' in between two movies that he was watching on TV.

Sunday morning

At 6:30 A.M. on that Sunday morning, Scotty went to the 'White Surf Ocean Front Hotel' Restaurant and had a good breakfast. While eating breakfast, he told himself that the woman he saw may have been visiting the area for the weekend only. Therefore, he would probably never see her again. Since his dreams of talking to her were shattered at this point, he decided to make reservations to catch a flight back home that Sunday afternoon. But before he did, he went for a walk on the beach one more time before getting a flight back home. It was now 7 A.M. As he walked south along the beach in front of Janelle's Vineyard area, a woman was coming in his direction. There were several couples and other single men and women walking on the beach that morning also. But, this woman 'caught his attention.' He knew that she was the same woman that he had seen the night before at midnight. She also had the same big Greyhound dog with her. As Scotty and the woman approached each other, she just happened to come close to him when he was walking toward her in the opposite direction.

Scotty looked over at the woman as she got close enough for him to speak. Then he said, "Excuse me. I am new in the area." She looked back at him as he said, "Can you tell me about some of the nicer restaurants in the area?" Since Scotty appeared to be a 'clean-cut' young man, the young woman did not see any harm in talking to him ...especially since it was only to answer his question. So, she told him about one of the best places to eat in the area. It was 'James and James' Fine Dining' which was located behind the hotel where he was staying. During the initial short time that she was talking to him, Scotty checked her ring finger and saw that she did not have any wedding rings on it. Of course he knew there could have been the possibility that she could have been married; but did not put her wedding rings on that early in the morning. Then Scotty quickly said, "I am Scotty John Williams. What is your name?" She said, "I am Celeste Jane Zetterower." "It is good to meet you Celeste," said Scotty. She did not respond back to him because she was not interested in continuing the conversation. But, since Scott thought there appeared to be a good rapport between them, he took advantage of the opportunity that he had. Of course, even though the opportunity was there, he did not want to overdo it. Also, Scotty wanted a chance to see Celeste again ...even it was just on the beach. Once again, he quickly said, "Do you walk here often?" Celeste said, "Yes, every morning." Celeste knew that Scotty was trying to get acquainted. She did not like to talk to strangers or anyone who was trying to get acquainted with her as fast as she felt that Scotty was trying too; but at the same time she did not want to be rude. Celeste looked at Scotty, and said, "I have to go." As Celeste walked away, Scotty said, "Okay. It is good to meet you." Celeste did not say anymore. She did not say, "It is good to meet you too." Apparently she thought that she had said too much already. So, she just looked back, smiled, and continued walking.

Went to the beach often

On Mondays, Wednesdays, and Thursdays, Celeste walked on the beach, and then go to her classes at school; but every weekend morning Celeste would take a stroll with her large Greyhound Dog, 'George III,' for about two miles on the six mile long public beach. Then, have the rest of the day to do whatever she wanted to. The wind would always be blowing in her beautiful long dark red hair. Most of the time when she went out on the beach with 'George III,' the sun had just come over the horizon from the East. As the glistening rays from the sun found their way to the ocean waves it created a radiant glow on Celeste's lovely face. She had been blessed with facial features that most women would have given anything to look as pretty as she did.

Scotty dismissed his earlier thoughts about flying back home that Sunday afternoon. He calls his manager, Joe Hazleton, again, and said, "Not only do I need that one day off that I talked to you about earlier; but can I have the rest of the week off and use the time as part of my vacation. Joe said, "You must be enjoying yourself or have you found a lady friend that you may be interested in?" Scotty laughed, and said, "It could be both." Joe laughed, too as he answered Scotty's question, and said, "Scotty, I want to enjoy yourself and have a good week." "Thanks. I will," said Scotty.

Another good free breakfast
He was there, too

On the next morning which was Monday, Scotty had a full breakfast of eggs, grits, bacon, two biscuits, and coffee at the 'White Surf Ocean Front Hotel' restaurant. Even though the special free breakfast that was included in Scotty's hotel rate for Saturday and Sunday morning, only the hotel manager gave the same free breakfast to Scotty one more morning on that following Monday.

Unknowing to Celeste, Scotty was out at that time of morning also. He had broken up with, Jennifer, the girl he was dating.

After Scotty had breakfast, he went to 'The Rock' area of the Kingleton Public Beach. On the morning before, he had talked briefly with Celeste as they came in opposite directions toward each other on the beach. He was hoping on this Monday morning to get, at least another glimpse of her as she walked up the beach.

When Scotty got to 'The Rock' area which had a high ridge overlooking the Kingleton Public Beach at the Atlantic Ocean, he sat on the same rock that he had sat on before when he first saw Celeste. Within minutes, as Scotty looked down over the rocks below, Celeste came walking by like she did every Monday morning. Once again, Scotty enjoyed seeing the wind blow through her beautiful long red hair that he had seen the day before when they had talked momentarily on the beach. The same thoughts that had lingered in his mind for several days about whether or not she was married came to him again. He just had to find out if she was married.

At different times for the next two mornings which were Tuesday and Wednesday, Celeste sees Scotty, and he sees her. For those two mornings, they only said, "Good morning to each other"...and nothing more. Scotty did not want to take away from the joy of the moment by just seeing her for two mornings in a row. So, he held his ground by not saying too much and by not appearing pushy and/or rushing too fast to get to knowing her.

He became bold and waited for her on the beach on the <u>third</u> morning

Scotty wanted to talk to Celeste. He knew her name now since he had met her earlier on the beach again. Also, he still knew that there was a possibility that she was married; but he wanted to be sure. She was too beautiful to not find out. On this third morning that he had seen Celeste, he walked toward her as she came walking up the beach. Celeste's dog, 'George III', started to growl; but she quickly got him to be silent.

They talk on the beach for a short time
They go to dinner together and talk more
She had a boyfriend

Celeste told him that she usually went walking early every morning. Then, she told him that she attended Royalton Agnes College on Mondays, Wednesdays, and Thursdays. She said that she could not talk long since she had a 10:00 A.M. class that morning.

Since Scotty knew that Celeste could not talk too long, he briefly told her that he was visiting the area for a week on vacation. Then he said, "There is something that I want to ask you. Are you married?" "No, I am not," said Celeste. Scotty followed up on her answer, and said, "Would you like to go to dinner with me this evening?" Since Celeste did not know Scotty too well, she just said, "Okay." If she had known him better, she would have probably said, "I'd love to." Scotty got Celeste's cell phone number, and they set the time for him to pick Celeste up so that they could go to 'Joe's Northern Bay Restaurant.'

Scotty and Celeste enjoyed themselves at 'Joe's Northern Bay Restaurant.' The food was very good, and they liked being in each other's company. Scotty really felt good about being with Celeste. In fact, he enjoyed every moment that he was with her, and it seemed that she felt the same way.

During their conversation at the restaurant, Celeste thought that she needed to tell Scotty about her boy friend, Don Holland So, at one point, she said, "There is something that I need to tell you. I have been seeing a young man in my life. His name is Don Holland. He will be out of town taking care of business this weekend and next weekend, too." "That is fine," said Scotty. "I am enjoying every moment of the time that you and I are together." "By the way, that brings me to my next question. I'd like to see you next weekend. Could I come up and enjoy the weekend with you?" "Sure." "That will be fine," said Celeste. Scotty was not going to allow Celeste saying that she was seeing Don to interfere with him and Celeste being together that weekend or the following one. Even though Celeste had told Scotty about Don Holland, he still wanted to see her again. Also, Scotty could only come up on weekends because he had to go back home to work on weekdays and he knew that Celeste had to go to school on Mondays, Wednesdays, and Thursdays. So the following weekend was perfect for both of them to be together and enjoy each other's company.

Notes:

Remember what Celeste had told herself earlier after her mother, Emily, left the family. Celeste said that she was going to find the man of her dreams, fall in love with him, and stay with him for the rest of her life. Of course, this did not mean that she would find the right man the first time that she met someone.

The second weekend after they met on the beach the second time

After Scotty and Celeste were together most of the following Saturday after he arrived that second weekend, Scotty suggested that they meet at 'The Rock' where he had seen her for the first time. He still cannot get her to be romantically involved with him because Celeste wants to be faithful in that regard to her boyfriend, Don Holland. Scotty and Celeste almost became close; but she hesitates.

Even though Celeste had told Scotty the first weekend that they were together at their first weekend Saturday dinner that she had a boyfriend, he was determined to get her to come 'in his direction.' Since he had got her cell phone number earlier, he called her when he got back home.

Notes:

Celeste could not see Scotty on the <u>third weekend</u> because Don Holland would be back.
She told Scotty that she had enjoyed his company during the time that they had together; but she would prefer <u>to not</u> continue the relationship.

Being with Scotty caused problems

Celeste told Don Holland about Scotty. She told him that she had just been with him for the two weekends after he met her (the weekend after he met her and the following weekend after that), and he would not be back. It made him feel better to a certain degree when she told him that she and Scotty were not romantically involved during that time.

After Scotty got back home from the second weekend that he was with Celeste, he called her every day. She asked him to not call her every day; but he refused to listen to her and still continued to call. One day when Scotty called, Don Holland asked Celeste, "I want to know who is calling you so often." Celeste told Don that it was Scotty.

Don became so jealous of Scotty that Celeste finally breaks up with him. He dates someone else to make her jealous; but it does not work.

Now, The Power Of Love Takes Over

One day when Scotty called Celeste, she told Scotty that she has broken up with Don, and they are not seeing each other anymore. Scotty immediately tells himself that things are now going good for him, and he needs to act quickly. After Celeste told Scotty that she had broken up with Don, Scotty said, "I d like to come up to visit you this coming Friday and see you for the entire weekend. Celeste thought for a moment. Then she said, "That will be fine." Scotty trying to keep his excitement down said, "See you then." "Okay," said Celeste. As they both turned off their cell phones, Scotty said to himself that he hoped to 'sweep Celeste off of her feet.'

Notes:

Celeste was really looking forward to seeing him; but she did not want him to know it at that point. She wanted to take it slow and easy as they got to knowing each other.

On the Friday of the weekend that Scotty was going to see Celeste after she broke up with Don, Scotty stayed at the 'White Surf Ocean Front Hotel' which was the first one that he stayed in when he first came to the area several weeks ago. The hotel was about a mile down the beach from where Celeste's Janelle Vineyard was located.

The chemistry between them is...

Scotty and Celeste enjoyed a very romantic Friday evening. On Saturday, they were together all day. In the evening on that Saturday, they went to 'The Rock.' This was where the serious romance began. Scotty found Celeste to be a very romantic woman. In fact, she was 'into the romance between them' more than any woman that he had been with or dated at any earlier time in his life. She was exactly what he wanted in a woman.

The midnight shadows of love
Romance between Scotty and Celeste

On the back side of 'The Rock' area just beyond the light house were trails that meandered through tall Oak Trees in a six area forest. The beautiful tall oak trees cast shadows of love between Scotty and Celeste that lingered throughout the night. It was bliss for both of them. The "light" stayed all night from the shadows of the early evening forms.

As two people who were really "in love" walked arm in arm, the lingering shadows began to fade into the night as daybreak appeared. The waves of the sea provided sounds of bliss on the surface of the smooth rock formations at 'The Rock' in the northern beach area. There were powerful feelings of love that could not be explained. It was definitely pure untainted love between them.

She tells him that he can stay in the cabin cruiser that Uncle Cecil left her

Later, in the evening, when Scotty took Celeste home where Courtney was still staying, he said, "I do not want to put a damper on a very romantic day and evening; but I wanted to share with you sometime about my late wife, Julie Lynn Williams, and what happened to her." Scotty briefly went over the things that he and Julie had experienced up to the time that she passed away. When he finished telling Celeste about Julie and her cancer, Celeste said, "I'm Sorry about what happened." "Well, I am sure that she would want me to find someone as loving and good as you." "Thank you Scotty," said Celeste." I love you." "I love you, too," said Scotty.

"By the way, I meant to tell you earlier. You are more than welcome to stay in the cabin cruiser starting tonight. In fact, I can go up there and help you get settled in." "Okay. But, I need to go and check out at the 'White Surf Ocean Front Hotel' and get my personal things from my room. I want you to go with me to the hotel to pick up my things." "I am right behind you. Let's go."

It was past midnight when Scotty and Celeste went to the 'White Surf Ocean Front Hotel.' They got Scotty's personal things from his hotel room. Then they went to the hotel lobby and checked out. Celeste helped Scotty make himself at home in the cabin cruiser. After they got the bed made and brought Scotty's personal things in, Scotty took Celeste back home. They kissed each other good night, and Scotty went back to the cabin cruiser.

They may not approve

Celeste told Courtney about Scotty. Courtney did not like the idea of Celeste dating someone whom she did not know that well … especially since he was from out of town. Courtney told Aunt Carol about Scotty. Aunt Carol and Courtney Anne both disagreed on Celeste dating, Scotty, the tall stranger.

Even though, Aunt Carol and Courtney were concerned about Celeste dating Scotty, Celeste made it very plain to them that see was going to keep seeing Scotty. So, neither Aunt Carol nor Courtney said anymore about it.

He came up from where he worked almost <u>every weekend</u>
The following things that they enjoyed doing together:

Every time they saw each other, the love, passion, and the attraction that was there left both of them breathless. Both Scotty and Celeste enjoyed going snorkeling in the water section of 'The Rock' area, going to the light House, riding in Celeste's cabin cruiser, riding horses, lying on the Kingleton Public Beach ...especially at night, building fires in fire places, swinging on porch swings, going for many walks, eating good food at good restaurants, and much more. In everything that they did, the romance was there every step of the way.

He got <u>a transfer</u> to her area

After coming up to see Celeste from Westbay, New Jersey for the third weekend, Scotty told Celeste that he was definitely interested in wanting to see her often and that he was 'falling in love' with her. She was probably 'falling in love' with Scotty too; but she did not want to be too forward and tell him at that point. On the week prior to the fourth weekend that Scotty comes up to see Celeste, he transfers from New Jersey Electric Power Company, the company that he worked for now, to a division of the same company in Morganton, New York. Both Scotty and Celeste were excited about the transfer. Now, they could be together and enjoy each other's company more than before.

Aunt Carol has the opportunity to get married

Aunt Carol Lynn McDora had been dating a man, Ken Elton Doyle, while Celeste was dating Scotty. She marries him and leaves Courtney and Celeste in the big condo.

'In-Love' with each other

After only two months of dating and being together, Scotty knew that Celeste was the one that he wanted to marry. Celeste was also thinking some similar thoughts. She said to herself that when Scotty asked her to marry him, she knew that she could fulfill the promise that she made to herself earlier when her mother, Emily, left them. The promise was that when she fell in love with a man like Scotty, she would stay with him forever. She knew that she was deeply in love with him.

Scotty's proposal

Two months after Scotty dates Celeste, he knows that he wants to propose to her. So, on the Saturday night exactly two months after he had his first dinner with Celeste, he took her out to 'Uncle James's Seafood and More Restaurant' in Blue Waters Ridge, New York. Immediately, after Scotty and Celeste were seated, Scotty said, "I need to go talk to the manager about something. I'll be back in a moment." Without questioning him about where he was going, Celeste said, "Okay." Scotty found out from a waitress that the manager's name was Allen Barton. The waitress went to the kitchen area where Allen was at the time, and said, "There is a gentleman out here who wants to talk to you." "Tell him I'll be there in a minute," said Allen. When Allen came out of the Kitchen, Scotty shook hands with Allen, and said, "Mr. Barton, I am Scotty Williams." Then Scotty gracefully looked over toward Celeste as he said, "I am going to propose to that beautiful and wonderful lady who is sitting over at that table this evening. When I get up from being on my knees after I propose to her, can you make an announcement that we are going to be married with no date set yet?" The young lady's name is Celeste Zetterower." "I'll take care of it," said Allen.

Scotty walked back over to Celeste, and said, "Sorry that it took so long." Celeste said, "That's okay." They ordered their meal and enjoyed the food, the small talk conversation, and just being together. When they finished eating, Scotty got up from his chair, looked at Celeste in a very romantic way, walked over to her, got on his knees, and said, "Celeste, I love you more than words can express. I want you to be with me for the rest of our lives." "Will you marry me?" With tears in her eyes, Celeste looked straight at Scotty, and said, "I love you, and I want to be with you. Yes, I will marry you." Scotty put the engagement ring on Celeste's wedding finger. Then, as Scotty got up off of his knees, Celeste pushed her chair back from the table and turned toward Scotty. She came close to him and they both embraced tightly; but at the same time gently. As Allen made the announcement of Scotty's proposal of marriage to Celeste, everyone in the restaurant clapped their hands and cheered for them. Scotty and Celeste kissed each other very passionately. It was a kiss that caused Scotty to have feelings of love like he had never had before. As they walked hand in hand out of the restaurant, Scotty looked over to Allen and said, "Thank you." Allen smiled, and said, "Congratulations." Scotty took Celeste back to the condo and shared the good news with Courtney. Courtney was extremely excited for them. She said, "Congratulations to both of you."

She's dating, too
The real estate deal

Courtney had been dating someone during the same time that Scotty and Celeste were dating. Courtney fiancé had just proposed to her on the day before. She told Celeste, "Even though I am extremely excited about it, both of us have been so busy with our busy schedules that I have not had time to tell you about it." "That is okay," said Celeste. Both Scotty and Celeste congratulated Courtney. It was a very happy day for everyone.

On the next Tuesday, Courtney asked Celeste if she could purchase Celeste's interest in the condo that Uncle Cecil gave them. Celeste said, "You can, and I'll make you a deal that you cannot turn down." In the agreement with Celeste, Courtney paid Celeste $1 and specified the term 'other considerations' in the transaction. The phrase 'other considerations' is used sometimes in that type of business deal.

Both Celeste and Courtney get married to their fiancés <u>on the same day</u>
Courtney and her husband live in the condo

Both weddings were the best ones that anyone had ever attended.

Cannot have children???
Now I am that way
Then there were three
Aunt Carol comes to 'Baby-Sit'

Part of the following scenario happened in real life

Before their marriage, Scotty and Celeste talked about wanting to have children. During their honeymoon and for a few months after returning home from their honeymoon, Celeste did not become pregnant. After six months, she told Scotty that she wanted to make an appointment with their new family doctor, Doctor King and talk to him about it. On that visit to Doctor King, Celeste finds out that she may not be able to have children.

Over the next few days, Celeste and Scotty talked about Celeste not being able to have a child. Both of them wanted children. So, they decided to adopt, Curt Preston Williams, a young boy. Aunt Carol comes over to 'Baby-Sit' with Curt while Scotty and Celeste are at work. Then she goes back home to be with her husband, Ken Elton Doyle.

Shortly after the adoption, Celeste finds herself pregnant with twin boys. Now, she and Scotty were going to have three wonderful boys. The two twins were named Alex Hans Williams and Travis Tray Williams. Carol McDora 'baby-sat' with all three baby boys.

Later, Celeste wanted to have a girl. She succeeds with one more pregnancy, and had a beautiful red headed girl. Celeste now had a daughter, Terri Emily, with the same color hair as hers. Carol 'baby-sat' with all four children.

Section Three

The Opposite Sides Of The Coin

The three murders happened about <u>nine years</u> ago
She is now <u>twenty four</u>
Celeste becomes <u>District Attorney</u> for the State of New York

After Celeste graduated from the Royalton Agnes College that she was going to and passed the bar exam to become an attorney, she decided to go one step further and run in the upcoming election that was going to be held in two weeks for the Office of District Attorney in the State of New York. Celeste ran for the D.A. Office and got it. She became the District Attorney for New York out of two other candidates. She felt that her excellent grade point average of 4.0 in her overall curriculum in school and her high score on the bar exam helped her get the votes that she needed to win the election.

Now that Celeste was District Attorney for the State of New York, she thought about trying to open the 'cold case' of the three murders committed that had been dormant for twelve years. Celeste wanted to see that justice was done in the murder case involving her dad. She made an appointment to talk to a panel of New York government officials about her opening the 'cold case.' She told the panel members that she believed she could produce evidence to show who the murdered all three men. The panel members said that no one had solved the case before; but they were willing to let her try to see what she could do with the case. They made one stipulation. Celeste only had one year to solve it. According to the government officials, they would give her the funds that she needed and the backing from several attorneys under her authority to go through every aspect of new leads and new evidence to help completely solve the case within that one year's time frame.

Celeste thanked the New York government officials for giving her permission to open the 'Cold Case' that no one had solved earlier. They knew that Celeste had the training to take over the 'cold case' and maybe solve it.

Notes:

Celeste had vowed earlier that she was going to find out who murdered her dad. Now, she was given the opportunity to go 'full speed' ahead with her energy and ability.

Celeste Takes Full Charge of the 'Cold Case'

Laying out a plan
Problems with the interviews

The first thing that Celeste wanted to do was to set up an outline of steps in an overall plan to help her solve the case in the time allotted by the State of New York government officials.

Celeste's first step was to visit Sherry and ask her some questions. Sherry very reluctantly met with Celeste and refused to answer any questions. She told Celeste that the murders happened a long time ago, and the case did not need to be opened now. Celeste did not say anything; but proceeded to give Sherry a subpoena to appear in court.

The next person that Celeste wanted to talk to was Betty from the restaurant. Betty told Celeste that she did not know anything about what happened. Even though Betty seemed to not know anything about the murders, Celeste gave her a subpoena to appear in court.

A few days later after talking to Betty, Celeste thought about talking to Doctor Matt Kevin Lancaster. Doctor Lancaster was now her personal doctor since Doctor King, the doctor that she had been going to, was murdered. Both Doctor Lancaster and Doctor King had been good friends and close acquaintances. At an earlier time just before Doctor King was murdered, Celeste felt that he wanted to tell her something when she went to him for her yearly physical several months ago; but it seemed that he could not get up the courage to do it. He would start off by saying, "I need to tell you something very important about Jim Al Benefer and your mother, Emily." Then, he said, "I cannot tell you about it." Celeste thought that it was something relating to Jim and Emily's marriage. She thought that she knew enough about that. So, at that time she did not think anything about what he was trying to tell her. Now, after both Doctor King and Jim had been murdered, Celeste knew that what he was trying to tell her probably had something to do with the individual(s) who murdered them. Since both doctors were close friends, Celeste thought that Doctor King may have told Doctor Lancaster what he was trying to tell her which was probably something about the murders. So, she made a decision to see Doctor Lancaster.

On the next morning after Celeste talked to Betty, she made an appointment to see Doctor Lancaster. When she made the appointment, she told his receptionist that it pertained to her talking to him about the three murders that happened nine years ago. The receptionist called Doctor Lancaster on his extension. She told him what Celeste wanted to make an appointment to talk about. He very bluntly told his receptionists that he did not want to take time to discuss anything about the murders with Celeste. The receptionist told Celeste that Doctor Lancaster had nothing to say in regard to the three murders. Celeste told the receptionists that she would come by the office and give Doctor Lancaster a subpoena to appear in court since he did not want to cooperate now. Within minutes, Celeste arrived at the doctor's office and asked the receptionists to get Doctor Lancaster to come to the reception area so that she could give him the subpoena. With a dismal look on his face, Doctor Lancaster took the subpoena that Celeste gave him and walked back into the exam room area.

Celeste left Doctor Lancaster's office and went straight home. Scotty was already home from work when she entered the front door. They hugged each other, and had a quick kiss. Scotty asked Celeste, "Did you have a good day?" "Yes," said Celeste. "But, some things came to my mind on the way home about the murders. I know I do not need to bring my work home with me; but this is something that has to be done now before I forget it. I'm sorry. It will only take a few minutes." "That is okay," said Scotty. "I understand." Celeste quickly went into the office area of their home, and started typing information related to her following thoughts. She knew that Doctor Lancaster might know something about the murders because he knew Doctor King who was the third person murdered and who was also the family doctor for Celeste and all of her family earlier. Not only did both doctors know each other, but they were very good friends. Doctor King was also Jim Al Benefer's doctor.

Celeste asked herself if Jim could have disclosed anything to Doctor King that might be evidence which could be used in court to convict the guilty person who murdered the three men. If Doctor Lancaster knew anything about the murders from Doctor King, Celeste intended to do everything she could to get Doctor Lancaster to disclose it in the first preliminary trial.

After typing the above thoughts on her computer, Celeste decided to save them in a new file on her computer. Then she started another file on her computer and put together a list of witnesses that she wanted at the first preliminary trial. She basically wanted Sherry, Betty, Doctor Lancaster, and maybe one or two other people who worked at the restaurant when Randy and Jim died. Celeste typed in the names of the witnesses in that special file, turned off the computer, and went to spend an enjoyable evening with Scotty and the three boys.

On the next morning, Celeste checked with the Superior Court to get them to set a date for the trial relating to the three murders. At this point, she did not have any evidence.

Larry V. Johnson

The First Preliminary Trial In Morganton, New York

Preface For This Section

The following courtroom scenes may <u>not</u> be true to real courtroom trials
The scenes have only been presented <u>as they relate to this story</u>

The battle between the sisters
Opposite sides of the coin

Courtney Anne who has become a counselor helps her mother, Emily, in her mental and emotionally state of mind.

Celeste has a degree in Criminal Justice. Both sisters compete with what they have to do on <u>opposite sides of the coin</u>.

The First Trial Began On A <u>Thursday</u>

<u>Notes</u>:

Even though an attorney was not needed in the first trial, one was added to this story.

<u>Mr. Tom Jeff Sanders</u> is the attorney

95

Celeste called the following people to the stand in the first preliminary trial

Sherry Cora Eubanks
Betty Jane Murphy from the restaurant
Monica Diane Hawkins who knew Randy and Emily
Doctor Lancaster
Patricia Melissa Morgan

Everyone stood as Judge Richard Anthony Lanier entered the court room. Then they sat down as he made himself comfortable in his executive chair.

Judge Richard Lanier looked toward Mrs. Celeste Zetterower-Williams, and said, "Mrs. Zetterower-Williams, who is your first witness?"

"Your **honor, I call Mrs. Sherry Eubanks to the stand**."

After Mrs. Eubanks was 'sworn in' Celeste began the questioning, and said, "Mrs. Eubanks, were you and Emily good friends?" "We knew each other, and yes we were very good friends." "Were you close enough that you shared many personal things with her?" "No. Not everything." Did she ever share anything with you about her relationship with her second husband Mr. Jim Al Benefer?" "Yes, she shared some things with me concerning Mr. Benefer." "I have no further questions at this point," said Celeste.

Judge Richard Lanier looked at the defense attorney, and said, "Is there any cross-examination Mr. Sanders?"
Mr. Sanders responded, "No, your Honor."

"I call Mrs. Betty Jane Murphy to the stand."

Then Celeste began the questioning. "Mrs. Murphy, you are employed as a waitress at Emily's Steak and Pizza House. Is that correct?" "Yes." "Were you there in the restaurant when all three murders were committed?" "No. I was only there when Mr. Randy Zetterower and Mr. Jim Al Benefer were murdered." "Were you in the kitchen area at any time before each one was served food?" "Yes. But not for any length of time." "Since I am a waitress, I stay on the floor taking orders and taking food to customers. At any time before those two murders, did you see anything different going on in the backroom that was not normal for the basic operation of the restaurant?" "No." "I have no further questions."

Judge Richard Lanier looked at the defense attorney, and said, "Is there any cross-examination Mr. Sanders?" "Not at this time, your Honor."

Mrs. Hawkins vouched for Emily being a good person and a good citizen in the community

"I call Mrs. Monica Diane Hawkins to the stand."

Then Celeste began the questioning. "Mrs. Hawkins, how long have you known Mrs. Emily Benefer?" "I have know her for about nine years this coming May." "How would you describe Mrs. Benefer's character?" "I find Mrs. Benefer to be a good citizen in today's society. She is a good role model, not only for adults, but for young people who are just starting out in the world on their own. I highly recommend Emily as a good business person." "Thank you, Mrs. Hawkins."

Judge Richard Lanier looked at the defense attorney, and said, "Is there any cross-examination Mr. Sanders?" "No, your Honor."

"I call Doctor Lancaster to the stand."

"Doctor Lancaster, did you know the late Doctor King?" "Yes, I did. I had an office on the West side of Morganton, New York. Since we were both internal medicine doctors, we had many things in common and a lot to talk about." "I know that you cannot disclose any personal information about patients that you see in your practice without a court order or under excruciating circumstances. But since this is a murder trial, I want you to answer the following question. Did the late Doctor King ever disclose to you anything about Mr. Randy Zetterower or Mr. Jim Benefer before he was murdered or who he thought murdered them?" "No, he did not." "Nothing, at all?" "No, nothing at all." "I have no further questions for this witness."

Judge Richard Lanier looked at the defense attorney, and said, "Is there any cross-examination Mr. Sanders?"
"No, your Honor."

"I call Patricia Melissa Morgan to the stand."

Then Celeste began the questioning. "Mrs. Morgan, I talked to you several days ago. At that time you stated that you were a waitress on duty when all three murders happened in 'Emily's Steak and Pizza House.' Is that correct?" "Yes, that is correct." "Before or after any of the three murders, did you see any one doing something different or suspicious in the backroom or anywhere else in the restaurant?" "No. As a waitress, I have to be on the floor in the restaurant most of the time waiting on and helping the restaurant patrons. So, I do not get a chance to see too much of what goes on in the backroom. The only person that I saw come in the back door of the restaurant after the murders was Mrs. Emily Benefer." "You do not think that that was unusual for her to come in immediately after each murder?" "No, I do not because she was always coming in and out of the restaurant throughout the day."

At that point, Mr. Sanders spoke up, and said, "Your honor. This is strictly speculation. Mrs. Emily Benefer is not on trial here. Judge Lanier said, "Please strike the last question from Mrs. Zetterower-Williams and the last answer from the witness. Mrs. Zetterower-Williams, would you be careful in your questioning." "I will your honor."

Notes:

Since Emily was not a suspect, and therefore was not on trial, Celeste could not allow Mrs. Morgan to reveal what she saw that day.

Judge Richard Lanier looked at the defense attorney, and said, "Is there any cross-examination Mr. Sanders?"
"No, your Honor."

Today was Thursday
Recess until 10:00 A.M. on <u>Tuesday</u>

Judge Richard Lanier hammered his **gavel** on his bench, and said, "We will have a 'Recess' until Monday at 10:00 A.M."

He called Mrs. Celeste Zetterower-Williams

Later after the first trial on Wednesday, Doctor Lancaster called Celeste on her cell phone and said, "I have obtained an important note from Doctor King's wife, Mary. According to the note, which I should not have read, Doctor King said that Jim knew the person who murdered Randy. The information further states that the name of the person who murdered Randy is revealed in another envelope. I called Mrs. King and asked her if she had the other envelope. She said that she had it; but the late Doctor King said for her to give that envelope in the locked box only to the District Attorney at the trial of the murders ...if one was conducted. I could not give you that note at the first trial because I did not have it then. In fact, I did not know anything about it until Doctor King's wife, Mrs. Mary Jane King, called me. She gave me a sealed envelope that Doctor King told her not to open. She said that he instructed her to give it to me or the police authorities if anything happened to him. Later, when she saw in the local newspaper about the trial of Mr. Randy Zetterower, Mr. Jim Benefer, and her late husband, Doctor King, being held here in Morganton, New York, she called me." "That is okay," said Celeste. "Thank you for telling me about those two envelopes. We will probably use the first envelope with the note in it along with the second one in the third trial." There may not be enough information presented in the second trial to definitely state that person's name ...even though it is in the second envelope.

Doctor Lancaster continued the conversation, and said, "The person who murdered Mr. Randy Zetterower probably murdered Mr. Jim Benefer and Doctor King also. They probably found out that Jim had told Doctor King who murdered Randy. So, they murdered both of them."

Doctor Lancaster did not want to hurt his practice in 'Internal Medicine' as a Family doctor, and he did not want to be involved anymore than he had to. So, he quickly asked Celeste, before she terminated the call, "Can I meet with you on Friday since I do not have my medical practice open on that day? I only have my medical practice open four days a week." Celeste said, "I can meet you at 'Uncle Bill's Grill' at 9:00 A.M. on Friday morning so that we can discuss the information in the note further." "Okay," said Doctor Lancaster. "I'll be there. I can also give you the note so that I can be completely out of the picture." "Well, you won't be completely out of the picture," said Celeste. "But, giving me the note will help with the evidence that we need."

Notes:

When Jim went to see Doctor King on an office visit one day before Jim was murdered, he told Doctor King some things about Randy's murder, but he was afraid to talk to the police authorities about it then. All of this information was typed on paper in the form of notes by Doctor King. After Doctor King typed the notes, he placed the paper with the notes on it in an envelope which he sealed and gave to his wife, Mary Jane King.

Larry V. Johnson

It Could Have Been The Fourth Murder

Their Saturday Routine

Having breakfast at 'Emily's Steak and Pizza House'

On the <u>Saturday morning</u> after the first trial, Doctor Lancaster and his wife, Jan Alice, decided to go to 'Emily's Steak and Pizza House' for breakfast. They had been there several times before, and enjoyed the food.

The incident
Emily's very, very close friend

Susan Janice Simmons, who worked with Doctor Lancaster on Monday through Thursday of each week and with Mrs. Emily Benefer on weekends, was one of Mrs. Benefer's closest friends. Mrs. Simmons knew when Doctor Lancaster got Doctor King's papers that Doctor King had typed up regarding what Jim had told him about Mr. Randy Zetterower's murder from Mrs. Mary King, Doctor King's wife. Since the information in the papers probably pertained to Mrs. Benefer, Susan told her about them.   Mrs. Benefer felt that there may be information in the papers that would hurt her and her business ...especially if she became a prime suspect not only to Mr. Randy Zetterower's murder, but to the other two murders also.

Mrs. Benefer knew that Doctor Lancaster and his wife came to the restaurant almost every Saturday for breakfast. She thought about checking to see if they were there on that particular Saturday morning. When she looked out through the small glass area near the top of the two doors that led to the kitchen and the backroom, she saw them sitting at a table in the middle of the restaurant. Mrs. Benefer checked Doctor Lancaster's order and saw that eggs were a part of his breakfast. She went into her office, got a syringe from her desk, put poison in it and walked over to where the eggs were in the restaurant refrigerator. Then she took out two eggs from the refrigerator, walked into a room through an open space that had no door on it and placed the eggs on a table in a corner of the room. This small room was almost never used by any of the restaurant employees except in emergencies when they accidently cut one of their fingers or other areas of their hand. Mrs. Benefer quickly looked around to see if anyone was in the area watching her. She told herself that all of the waitresses were either out on the floor or going to the kitchen area to pick up orders. As she carefully picked up one egg at a time and injected the poison through the egg shell of each egg with the poison filled syringe, Mrs. Rhonda Powell was going through the far side of the other room. Mrs. Benefer was so busy in her thoughts about what she was doing that she failed to see Mrs. Powell, one of the waitresses, go by on the other side of the big room adjacent to the small room. Mrs. Powell saw Mrs. Benefer putting something in a syringe. Quickly and quietly as she could without letting Mrs. Benefer see her, Mrs. Powell went back into the kitchen area next to the room that she was going through, picked up an order of food that was ready and took it out to a customer on the floor. She did this so that if Mrs. Benefer saw her at that time, she would think that Mrs. Powell was only working and not spying on her. Mrs. Benefer walked out to the kitchen with the two eggs in her hand shortly after Mrs. Powell took the food order to the customer. She went over to, Jimmy Dale Reese the cook, and said, "I want to cook these eggs for Doctor Lancaster. He is my special guest today, and I want to do the honors of cooking part of his breakfast." "Okay," said Jimmy.

During all of this time, Mrs. Rhonda Powell was watching every move that Mrs. Benefer was making. Mrs. Powell knew that Mrs. Benefer had put something in the eggs; but she did not know what had been injected into them. She was not taking any chances about whether or not it was harmful. When Mrs. Powell picked up the breakfast in the kitchen to take to Doctor Lancaster and his wife, Jan, Mrs. Benefer said, "Make sure that Doctor Lancaster gets the plate on the left side of the tray with the eggs on it. He is my special guest today, and I wanted to cook them for him." Mrs. Powell said, "Okay, I'll take care of it."

Mrs. Powell casually took Doctor Lancaster and Jan's food them at their table where they were sitting. She looked at Doctor Lancaster, and said, "Do not eat the eggs; but act like you are eating the other food. As Doctor Lancaster and Jan looked toward Rhonda in a questioning demeanor, Rhonda said, "Please trust me. I saw Mrs. Benefer put something in your eggs, and I feel that something is wrong with them. Then she told Doctor Lancaster that she was going to call the police immediately and for him to fall to the floor as if he were dying. Doctor Lancaster agreed to do everything that Rhonda said for him to do.

Just as the doctor simulated falling out of his chair onto the restaurant floor, Rhonda called 911 and briefly told the operator that she saw Mrs. Emily Benefer put something in Doctor Lancaster's eggs. Then Rhonda hung up and did not reveal her name so that the call could not be traced back to her. Mrs. Benefer thought that Doctor Lancaster had actually been harmed by what she put in the eggs. So, she quickly went out the back door of the restaurant with the syringe in her hand and threw it into the big restaurant dumpster.

While Mrs. Benefer was getting rid of the syringe, Mrs. Powell got the eggs and put them in some aluminum foil so that she could give it to the police later. Then, Doctor Lancaster and his wife, Jan, paid their bill and left before the police arrived. When Mrs. Benefer came back into the restaurant, she was shocked that Doctor Lancaster and his wife, Jan, had left. She knew then that something had gone terribly wrong with what she had planned. So, she quickly went out the back door and left just before the police arrived.

Two policemen arrived within about three minutes of the time that Mrs. Powell had called them. Mrs. Powell went over to them, and said, "I may be mistaken; but I have the eggs here in some aluminum foil that I saw Mrs. Benefer put something into them. I saw her do the same thing to Mr. Randy Zetterower, Mr. Jim Benefer and Doctor King's food before they were murdered. So, when I saw her inject something into Doctor Lancaster's eggs, I thought that I had better warn him. One of the police officers said, "I need to talk with Mrs. Benefer." "She left after Doctor Lancaster fell out of his chair," said Mrs. Powell. The police took the egg sample to the New York Crime Lab.

Notes:

Doctor Lancaster was almost murdered at Emily's restaurant in the same way as the other three men.

The police took the egg remains in some aluminum foil to the New York Crime Lab. The New York Crime Lab was not usually open on Saturday. But, the police officers wanted to get the results from the eggs immediately. Rhonda had told them that she saw Mrs. Benefer put something with a syringe into all three of the other men's food who were murdered in Emily's restaurant. The police officers knew that Emily may tie into all three earlier murders that happened in her restaurant as well as the one that appeared to be attempted with Doctor Lancaster on that Saturday. They now knew this because of what Rhonda had seen Mrs. Benefer do with all three previous murders as well as with her apparent attempt to put something, which may have been harmful, in Doctor Lancaster's eggs. Also, Mrs. Benefer leaving the scene at the restaurant immediately when she saw that Doctor Lancaster had walked away from his table unharmed was another reason that they wanted to find out what was in the eggs. They wanted to get the results of what was in the eggs before Mrs. Benefer had a chance to get to far away. The police knew from media reports of the trial that was going to take place regarding the three murders that happened at Emily's restaurant. They knew that Celeste was the 'District Attorney' For the State Of New York and that she was handling the trial. The police called Celeste and told her everything. Due to her authority and power, Celeste arranged for the New York Crime Lab to come to the lab on that Saturday and work on finding out immediately the substance that had been injected into the eggs. The New York Crime Lab found a poison in the eggs which would have been fatal to Doctor Lancaster if he had eaten them. The lab called Celeste and told her the results of their findings. Celeste called the Morganton, New York Police Department and had them put out a warrant for Mrs. Emily Benefer's arrest. The police authorities sent out an 'All Points Bulletin' (APB).

Arrested and taken to jail without bond

Mrs. Susan Simmons, Mrs. Benefer's confidant, who worked in Mrs. Benefer's restaurant on weekends, wanted to help Mrs. Benefer. Unknowingly to Mrs. Powell, Mrs. Susan Simmons saw Mrs. Powell spying on Mrs. Benefer when Mrs. Benefer was putting the poison into Doctor Lancaster's eggs.

In the afternoon on the same day that Mrs. Benefer was arrested, Mrs. Powell was getting some food from the restaurant freezer. It was the weekend when Mrs. Simmons was there at the restaurant. Mrs. Simmons followed Mrs.

Powell to the freezer at a distance so that Mrs. Powell would not know that she was being followed. Just as Mrs. Powell opens the freezer door, Mrs. Simmons knocks Mrs. Powell over the head, pushes her into the freezer, and locks the freezer door.

She survived

Shortly after Rhonda was locked in the restaurant freezer, Jane Mac Intosh went to the freezer to get some food to be cooked for the dinner meals later on that same day. She saw Mrs. Powell in the freezer. She pulled her out of the freezer onto the floor of the restaurant and ran to the kitchen to get someone to help her. Betty was on duty that day, and she called 911 for an ambulance. The ambulance took Mrs. Powell to the Morganton, New York Hospital where she recovered. The Hospital staff said that if Mrs. Powell had been in the freezer for two more hours, she would not be alive then.

Celeste knew that Susan kept Mrs. Benefer posted on everything that concerned Mrs. Benefer. Susan knew that Rhonda had told Celeste about Emily putting something in Doctor Lancaster's eggs. Therefore Susan was probably the one who put Rhonda in the restaurant freezer. She was trying to keep Rhonda from testifying or revealing any more information that might hurt Emily. After thinking those thoughts, Celeste decided that she needed to go by 'Emily's Steak and Pizza House' late that Saturday afternoon just before the dinner meals were served at 7:00 P.M. to give Susan a subpoena in person to appear at the second trial.

The Second Trial On Tuesday

The second trial was on a Tuesday after the week of the first trial
Also, another doctor appointed to the case by the State of New York

Doctor Hayley Joel Grindle is the new doctor appointed by the State of New York to work with Celeste and the court in the solving of the murders. His main task was to assist in the medical part of the case involving the poisoning of the three men. Doctor Grindle obtained a copy of Doctor King's papers that would be used as evidence in the case from Celeste. Celeste had got the papers from Doctor King's wife, Mary Jane King.

Doctor Grindle had been appointed to the case because Doctor Lancaster did not want the trial to affect his private practice as a medical doctor ...especially since he was involved with receiving Doctor King's papers as evidence in Mr. Randy Zetterower's murder.

Three doctors were involved

For those who are keeping track of the story, there were three doctors involved in this murder case. Doctor King was the one who was murdered; Doctor Lancaster was the one that did not want to destroy his practice; and Doctor Grindle was appointed by the State of New York to take over in the final trials.

The Second Trial Begins

Mrs. Celeste Zetterower-Williams called the following people to the stand

Sherry Cora Eubanks
Betty Jane Murphy, <u>the</u> waitress from the restaurant
Rhonda Angela Powell, a waitress at the restaurant
Doctor Hayley Joel Grindle
Susan Janice Simmons
Emily Mae Benefer

It was 9:30 A.M. on a Tuesday morning. Celeste and Courtney arrived in separate cars at the Morganton Court House. Both of them met in the hallway just outside the courtroom where the trial was going to be held. They briefly discussed some preliminary information regarding the case. After the discussion they walked into the courtroom. Courtney went into the area where visitors and spectators sat. Celeste sat at a table on the right side of the court room facing the Judge's bench.

Brought to trial

Mrs. Emily Mae Benefer was brought in with a police woman. The police woman and Mrs. Benefer were seated at a table on the left facing the judge's bench.

At 10:00 A.M. the second trial began

Everyone stood as Judge Richard Lanier came into the court room. Then, everyone sat down. Judge Lanier looked toward Celeste, and said, "Mrs. Zetterower-Williams, who is your first witness?"

I call Mrs. Sherry Cora Eubanks to the stand."

Celeste began the questioning. "Mrs. Eubanks, did you meet with Emily at anytime on that Saturday morning?" "Yes, I did meet her." "Where did you meet her?" "I met her at the Birdsong Building." "How did you know where to meet her?" "She called me the Friday evening at my home before she left Mr. Randy Zetterower and the girls on the following Saturday morning." "Did she say anything to you about anything other than where she was to meet you?" "Yes." "What else did she tell you?" "Then she said that she was going to meet Mr. Jim Al Benefer before she met me at 10:00 A.M. at the Birdsong Building." "Did she tell you her reasons for meeting Mr. Benefer?" "No she did not." "Did she ever say anything to you about leaving Randy, Courtney, and Celeste on that particular Saturday morning?" "Yes. Earlier in the week, before that Saturday when she left them, she told me that she was going to leave her husband, Randy, and her two daughters, Courtney and Celeste, on the following Saturday to be with Jim Al Benefer whom she met while in high school. She also said that she wanted me to understand that she and Jim were not going to be living together. Then she said that over the last few weeks each one of them had found a separate place to stay until she got a divorce from Randy so that she and Jim could get married."

"I have no further questions from this witness; but I reserve the right to call her back," said Celeste.

Judge Richard Lanier looked at the defense attorney, and said, "Is there any cross-examination Mr. Sanders?" "No, your Honor."

Celeste looked toward the spectators, and said, "Your Honor, **I call Mrs. Betty Jane Murphy to the stand**."

111

Mrs. Murphy was sworn in. Then Celeste began the questioning. "Mrs. Murphy, was Jim Al Benefer the manager of 'Emily's Steak and Pizza House' on the day that Randy was murdered as well as after Randy was murdered up until the time that he was also murdered?" "Yes. He was the manager." "Did Jim leave the restaurant before or after Randy's food was prepared …on the day that Randy was murdered?" "Mr. Jim Benefer left before Randy's food was prepared." "Was Emily there at any time on that same day?" "No. She was not there."

Judge Richard Lanier looked at the defense attorney, and said, "Is there any cross-examination Mr. Sanders?"
"No, your Honor."

I call Mrs. Rhonda Angela Powell to the stand."

Celeste said, "Mrs. Powell, do you work at Emily's Steak and Pizza House?" "Yes, I do." "What is your position there?" "I am a waitress." "I want you to tell the court what you saw in the backroom and in the office of the restaurant on the same day just before Mr. Randy Zetterower was murdered." "I saw Mr. Jim Benefer go out the back door of the restaurant. Did he leave before Mr. Randy Zetterower was served his food or after he was served? It was several minutes after Randy was served. Then what happened after he left. He went over to a car that was parked over toward the back of the restaurant property. There was a woman inside with sun glasses on. At that point, I could not tell anything about the woman. They talked for a minute. Then Mr. Benefer went over to his car, got in, and drove off. Then, the woman in the car came in the back door of the restaurant. She was still wearing sun glasses. Since I was working as a waitress, I was okay when I observed what she was doing. She did go into her office for about ten minutes, and then she left.

Notes:

Mrs. Powell had called Celeste earlier before the trial. She told Celeste that she had some important information about what happened on the day that Mr. Randy Zetterower was murdered. Then she said that she was afraid to come forward with the information until now. Celeste had met with Mrs. Powell earlier. Mrs. Powell told Celeste the exact opposite of what Mrs. Betty Jane Murphy has stated in her testimony to the court.

Rhonda's pictures entered as evidence
The pictures show Jim and Emily behind the restaurant on the day of Randy's murder

As Mrs. Celeste Zetterower-Williams walked back to a table where she was sitting earlier, the second trial began. She picked up an envelope on the table, and said, "With the court's permission, I want to enter this envelope with pictures of Mrs. Emily Benefer and Mr. Jim Benefer in it as 'Exhibit G'. The pictures were taken by Mrs. Rhonda Powell from a backroom window in 'Emily's Steak and Pizza House' on the day of Mr. Randy Zetterower's murder. This backroom window gave a good view of everything that was going on behind the restaurant."

"Now, Mrs. Powell, I want you to tell us how you managed to take these pictures of Mr. and Mrs. Benefer without them knowing about it."

Mrs. Rhonda Powell said, "I was getting off from work as Jim was going out the backdoor of the restaurant. So, I saw him leave, and therefore I knew the time that he left. I was a photographer part time, and I kept a camera in my car. When Jim left out the back door of the restaurant, I quickly clocked out, went to my car, got my camera, and went to a window in the back of the restaurant. The window gave me a clear view of everything that went on behind the restaurant." Rhonda continued, and said, "Unnoticed by Jim or Emily, I took pictures of every move they made.

Then after I took the pictures, I put the camera back in my car and locked the car. Then I walked rapidly back into the restaurant and to the back room where Emily had gone to. Emily saw me come in, and said to me, "It is past your scheduled work hours for today. Have you not clocked out?" "Yes, but, I forgot my lunch bag in the refrigerator. I had to come back and get it so that I can have something to put my lunch in for tomorrow." "Oh, okay that is fine." "Then, I said to Mrs. Benefer that I would see her tomorrow. Mrs. Benefer responded, and said, "Okay."

Celeste looked at Mrs. Powell, and said, "Thank you, Mrs. Powell." Then she turned toward Judge Lanier as she stated to him that she had no further questions of this witness.

Judge Richard Lanier looked at the defense attorney, and said, "Is there any cross-examination Mr. Sanders?" "No, your Honor."

Notes:

Due to the evidence that was being presented, Mrs. Celeste Zetterower-Williams made it a mandatory condition for Emily and Susan to be in the courtroom during the second trial. After Mrs. Powell gave her testimony about the pictures, Emily looked at Susan in the courtroom as if to say, why did you not tell me about this.

Susan usually worked on weekdays for Doctor Lancaster. But today, on Thursday, she was in the courtroom because she had been given a subpoena by Celeste to appear in court at the second trial of the three murders that happened at 'Emily's Steak and Pizza House.'

"I call Mrs. Murphy back to the stand."

"Mrs. Murphy, you just heard just a few minutes ago Mrs. Powell's testimony as to what really happened in the backroom of the restaurant as well as descriptive scenes of what happened behind the restaurant on the day that Mr. Randy Zetterower was murdered. Would you like to change your story? False testimony could be considered as 'contempt of court.'"

Tears came in Mrs. Murphy's eyes as she said, "Jim told me not tell anyone as to the time when he left the restaurant. I have stuck with that same story since the day that Mr. Randy Zetterower was murdered." "I want you to step down from the stand, and sit at the table that I am pointing to," said Celeste. Mrs. Murphy knew that she was going to be held for 'Contempt of Court' since she lied in her testimony.

Celeste looked toward Judge Lanier, and said, "Your Honor, I would like to have some time to talk to Mrs. Murphy about   evidence   pertaining   to   this   trial.

Judge Lanier said, "Granted! The court is in recess until Wednesday at 10:00 A.M."

When the court session was over, Celeste walked over to the table where she had told Mrs. Murphy to go to during the trial. Before Celeste could say anything about the 'Contempt' charges against her, Mrs. Murphy spoke up and told Celeste that she was the one who overheard Mr. Jim Benefer talking to someone on the phone. She said at that time she did not know that he was talking to Mrs. Emily Benefer. Celeste listened attentively to what Mrs. Murphy had to say about the cell phone conversation between Mr. Jim Benefer and Mrs. Emily Benefer. Then she made the decision that she would remove the contempt charges against Mrs. Murphy in exchange for her to testify against Mrs. Benefer later.

The trial opened again on Wednesday at 10:00 A.M. Celeste has Doctor King's notes entered as evidence

At this point in the trial, Celeste walked back over to the table where she was sitting again. This time she picked up a large envelope that contained Doctor King's notes relating to Mr. Randy Zetterower and Mr. Jim Benefer's murders. She looked at Judge Lanier, and said, Your Honor, I want to enter this envelope with notes in it as evidence relating to Mr. Randy Zetterower's murder, and we will call it 'Exhibit H'.

Then Celeste said, "I call Doctor Haley Joel Grindle to the stand."

After Doctor Grindle was 'sworn in,' Celeste began the questioning. "Doctor Grindle, you are a medical doctor, and you have had a private practice for fourteen years. Is that correct?" "Yes, that is correct," said Doctor Grindle. Celeste walked over to the table close to Judge Lanier's bench, picked up the envelope with the note in it, looked at Doctor Grindle, and said, "Do you recognize this envelope?" Doctor Grindle looked at it, and said, "Yes, I do." "Have you seen and reviewed Doctor King's note in this envelope which have been entered as evidence in this court relating to Mr. Randy Zetterower and Mr. Jim Benefer's murders?" "Yes, I have." Celeste put the envelope back on the table, and said, "I have no further questions of this witness at this time."

Judge Richard Lanier looked at the defense attorney, and said, "Is there any cross-examination Mr. Sanders?" "No, your Honor."

Celeste called Mrs. Susan Janice Simmons to the stand.

"Mrs. Simmons, do you work at 'Emily's Steak and Pizza House?'" "Yes, on weekends only." "Is this your only job?" "No." "Where else do you work?" "I worked with the late Doctor King. Now, I work with Doctor Lancaster." "When you worked with Doctor King, did you and Emily become close friends?" "Yes. Since she was a patient, we had the opportunity to have dinners together and discuss subjects close to both of us." "Did you ever discuss anything with Emily about her relationship with Jim?" "Yes, many times." "When Jim told Doctor King who he thought murdered Randy, did you tell Emily about that?" "Yes, I did." "What did she say when you told her?" "She said that was beginning to be a problem which she would take care of shortly."

Celeste continued, and said, Mrs. Simmons, you have stated in earlier testimony that you work for Doctor Lancaster Monday through Thursday, and you work for Mrs. Benefer on Saturday and Sunday. Is that correct?" "Yes, it is," said Mrs. Simmons. "Are you aware that the New York Crime Lab found poison in the eggs which Doctor Lancaster had been served with his breakfast last Saturday?" "No, I did not." "You did not know anything about it." "No."
"That is all I have for this witness," said Celeste. "But, I reserve the right to call her back."

Larry V. Johnson

Finally, Celeste called Emily Mae Benefer to the stand

Celeste looked at Judge Richard Lanier, and said, "I know that this is inappropriate, your honor; but I would like with the court's permission to call Mrs. Emily Zetterower-Benefer to the stand." "Do you have any objection, Mr. Sanders?" "No, your honor," said Mr. Sanders "Granted," said Judge Lanier.

Celeste looked at her mother, Emily, and said, "I call Mrs. Emily Mae Benefer to the stand."

Notes:

Emily became emotionally unstable as she walked up to the stand. Even though she had been able to elude the law enforcement officials to this point, she realized that the 'evidence was there to convict her.'

Intro to Celeste questioning Mrs. Emily Benefer

After Mrs. Emily Benefer was sworn in, Celeste began the questioning. "Mrs. Benefer, you are the owner of 'Emily's Steak and Pizza House.' Is that correct?" "Yes, that is correct." "Did you marry the late Mr. Jim Benefer and hire him to be manager of your restaurant?" "Yes, I did." "Was that your first marriage?" "No, it was not." "Who were you married to before you married Mr. Benefer?" "I was married to the late Mr. Randy Zetterower." "Isn't it true that you married Mr. Benefer immediately after Mr. Zetterower died?" "Yes." "Isn't it also true that, according to the 'New York Crime Lab,' Mr. Randy Zetterower was murdered by the effects of poison in your restaurant?" "Yes, that is true." "Two other men were murdered in your restaurant by the same method of poisoning over a two year period. They were your second husband, Mr. Jim Benefer and Doctor King ...who was your family doctor." "That is all I have for the witness. I reserve the right to call her back later."

Her initial feelings while on the stand

Mrs. Emily Benefer was emotionally unstable and not feeling well during the entire time that she was being questioned by Celeste Williams. Of course, she had been having those same problems of being emotionally unstable and not feeling well for the last few years. Her feelings of guilt that was beginning to surface and be exhibited now while she was on the witness stand may have also contributed to those two problems ...which were really minor. However, neither one of the two problems was serious enough to prevent her from standing trial for the three murders that she committed.

"I call Mrs. Sherry Cora Eubanks back to the stand."

"Mrs. Eubanks, you stated in your testimony earlier that Mrs. Emily Benefer called you on the Friday before the Saturday that she left Mr. Randy Zetterower and the girls, which included me, to tell you to meet her at the Birdsong Building. Is that correct?" "Yes. That is correct." "Mrs. Eubanks, when you met Mrs. Benefer on that Saturday morning at the Birdsong Building, during the course of the conversation, did she tell you anything that she discussed with Mr. Jim Benefer earlier that morning?" "No. She did not say anything." "Also, when Mrs. Benefer met with you that Saturday morning at the Birdsong Building, did it ever occur to you that she may have met with you so that she could have an alibi for her being with Mr. Jim Benefer earlier that morning before she met you?" "No, it did not. But, I do remember something she told me while we were talking. She said for me to tell anyone who asked me what time I met her at the Birdsong Building to say that I had been with her all morning." "Did that make you suspicious that she may have been trying to cover up something?" "No, Mrs. Benefer and I are good friends, and I wanted to do everything I could to help her in any way that I could ...without questioning the reason behind what she wanted me to do."

Celeste said, "That is all I have for this witness."

Judge Richard Lanier looked at the defense attorney, and said, "Is there any cross-examination Mr. Sanders?" "No, your Honor."

"I call Mrs. Emily Benefer back to the stand."

Celeste began the questioning. "Mrs. Benefer, I am going ask you questions about where you were <u>before</u> and <u>after</u> Mr. Randy Zetterower's murder in your restaurant."

The 'Alibi'

"Mrs. Eubanks stated in her earlier testimony that you told her you were going to meet Mr. Jim Benefer early on that Saturday morning when you left Mr. Randy Zetterower and the girls. In that same testimony she also stated that she did not know why you wanted to meet Mr. Jim Benefer, or why you met him so early. I want you to tell the court the reason that you met Mr. Benefer early on that Saturday morning." "In answer to both questions, I wanted to be with him," said Mrs. Benefer. "I think that it was more than you just wanting to be with him," said Celeste. I think that you and Mr Benefer made plans to get rid of Mr. Zetterower as soon as possible. Then, both of you could get married immediately ... which is what you actually did after Mr. Zetterower was murdered. At that point you were

121

madly in love with Mr. Benefer ...even though he may not have been that much in love with you.

The defense attorney, Mr. Sanders, interjected, and said, "Mrs. Williams, you have no proof of your statements."

Celeste responded, and said, "I have a witness to testify and tie all of the points that I am making together in a cell phone call. So, the statements that I am making here are facts."

Judge Lanier looked at Mr. Sanders, and said, "Overruled."

Celeste continued with Mrs. Emily Benefer's questioning, and said, "When you and Mr. Benefer met that Saturday morning, you did not want anyone tying you two together as the ones who were planning Mr. Randy Zetterower's fate. Therefore, you had Mrs. Sherry Eubanks meet you at the Birdsong Building just after you left Mr. Jim Benefer. Then according to Mrs. Eubank's testimony earlier, you told Mrs. Eubanks not to tell anyone that you were with her during the latter part of the morning only. You told her to tell anyone who asked when you two met that morning that both of you had been together all Saturday morning. This gave you an alibi so that no one would know that you and Jim had met to plan Mr. Randy Zetterower's fate. Since you and Mrs. Eubanks were very close friends, you did not think that she would ever tell the truth about what you told her to do regarding the time frame of how long you wanted her to say that both you and Mrs. Eubank's had been together that Saturday morning." "That is not true," said Mrs. Benefer.

"Now, I want to turn my questioning to the time that Mr. Jim Benefer left the restaurant on the day that Mr. Randy Zetterower was murdered. According to a statement by Rhonda, Jim, the manager of your restaurant, left just after Randy's food was prepared and served rather than before it was prepared and served. He met you in your car which was parked behind the restaurant. We know that was you in the car that was parked behind the restaurant from pictures taken by Mrs. Powell. You were in a disguise and had on sun glasses. Is this true?" "I do not know. I cannot remember. Many people park behind the restaurant. It could have been anyone." "But, as I just stated, we have pictures to prove that it was you in that car."

"Also, according to Mrs. Powell's testimony earlier, Jim was there in the restaurant when Randy's food was prepared and when it was served to him by the waitress Betty." In addition, Mrs. Betty Murphy saw you when you came in the back door of the restaurant shortly after Jim left. Her witness added to the pictures that Mrs. Rhonda Powell took puts you in a position of being more than a prime suspect.

My following questions are in regard to the cell phone call that Mr. Jim Benefer received when he started to go out the back door of 'Emily's Steak and Pizza Restaurant.' According to Mrs. Betty Murphy's testimony, Mr. benefer wanted to leave the restaurant before Randy was served his fateful meal; but he got a cell phone call that delayed him from leaving when he was supposed to. He asked Betty not to tell the actual time that he left because of the call that he answered just before he left. Was that call from you?" "I do not know anything about that," said Emily. We have a witness here in the court today to tell us that she overheard Jim talking to you on his cell phone.

"I have no further questions at this point of this witness."

Judge Richard Lanier looked at the defense attorney, and said, "Is there any cross-examination Mr. Sanders?" "No, your Honor."

Betty overheard the conversation

"I call Mrs. Betty Murphy back to the stand."

Mrs. Murphy, tell the court what you heard Mr. Jim Benefer say on his side of the cell phone conversation between him and Mrs. Benefer. "He said that it was done, and he was on his way to see her. He also said on that same call to her that the plans they made on the Saturday that she left Randy and the girls had been carried out as planned. Then he said that they could be married and live a happy life together.

Judge Richard Lanier looked at the defense attorney, and said, "Is there any cross-examination Mr. Sanders?" "No, your Honor."

(The above testimony was done by Mrs. Murphy so that she could get her 'Contempt of Court' charges dismissed.)

"I call Mrs. Emily Benefer back to the stand."

"Mrs. Benefer, would you like to change your answer about Mr. Benefer talking to you and no one else?" Shaking in her voice, Mrs. Benefer held to her previous statement, and said, "Mr. Benefer may have been talking to someone else. I do not know." Celeste continued, and said, "We have phone records to show that he was talking to you on your cell phone."

She did it

Emily was in the restaurant before Jim left. She was the one who put the poison in Randy's food with a syringe. Then she went back to her car behind the restaurant. No one saw her that time because she was very careful to come in without anyone noticing her like she did the second time that she came back in to get the syringe that she left in her office. Jim also helped her the first time that she came in by keeping all of the waitresses and cooks out on the floor of the restaurant for a big birthday party that was being celebrated by one of the restaurant customers.

Celeste questions Emily so intensely and brings out information involving Emily in all three murders that causes Emily to break down emotionally. At one point Emily started crying. Courtney stood to her feet, and spoke up, "Celeste, stop it." Judge Lanier told Courtney to sit down, and said, "Order in the court." Then he dismissed the court, and said, "A trial by jury will be held three months from now. The exact date of the trial will be announced within the next two weeks."

After that trial

After that particular court session where Celeste drilled Emily, to the point of Emily breaking down into tears, Courtney told Celeste, "You were too hard on Emily." "Maybe I was," said Celeste. "But, I had to get the answers about how the three murders were committed and the truth about why they were committed so that justice could be done.

Still in custody and not released

Emily was taken back to jail to wait for her murder trial three months later. Her third husband, Mr. Jesse Lee Wilbanks, hired a very good criminal attorney, Mr. John Reed, to represent her.

Larry V. Johnson

The Third Trial **<u>By Jury</u>**

Three Months Later

All three meet

Even though Celeste does not represent Emily in the case, she interviews Emily just before the third trial in Judge Lanier's chambers. Courtney, Mr. Reed, Emily's attorney, and Judge Lanier are in the same room during Celeste's interview. Emily was brought in by a police woman who stood at the door which had been closed by Celeste.

After Celeste's questions and Emily's answers at the end of an emotional second trial, Celeste knew that Emily was probably the one who murdered Mr. Randy Zetterower, Mr. Jim Benefer, and Doctor King. Celeste looked at Emily, and said, "There is a lot of evidence against you that is now showing beyond a reasonable doubt that you murdered all three victims in your restaurant. I do not know what the decision of the jury will be; but with the evidence against you, it does not look good." Then Celeste asked Emily, "Why did you do it?" Emily responded, and said, "People change as they go through life ...and especially when they fall 'in love' with one certain person like I did with Jim. Later, after I married him, I realized that he did not love me like I loved him. Celeste, I'm sorry for what I did to you and Courtney." "I am also sorry because of what I have to do," said Celeste. Celeste continued, and said, "I want you to remember that I still love you." "I love you and Courtney, too," said Emily.

Celeste and Courtney went back into the courtroom just before the third trial began. Celeste sat at a desk-like table on the right side of the courtroom. Emily was escorted by the woman police officer into the courtroom to sit next to her attorney, Mr. Allen Reed, at a desk-like table on the left side of the courtroom facing the judge's bench.

The Third Trial Begins

Mrs. Celeste Zetterower-Williams calls the following people to the stand

Mrs. Rhonda Powell
Mrs. Susan Janice Simmons
Doctor Grindle

Judge Lanier entered the courtroom from his chambers. Everyone stood up and then sat back down. As everyone was sitting down, Judge Lanier made himself comfortable in his chair, looked toward Mrs. Celeste Zetterower-Williams, and said, "Mrs. Williams. Who is your first witness?"

Celeste called Mrs. Rhonda Powell to the stand.

"Mrs. Powell, did you know Susan Simmons." "Not personally." "We worked together at the restaurant." "Did you ever see Mrs. Simmons go into Emily's office?" "Yes." "Was it often?" "Yes." "Were you working in the restaurant as a waitress before each one of the three murders?" "Yes, I was there." "Did you see Susan going into Emily's office just before each murder?" "Yes, I did. Just before Mr. Randy Zetterower and Mr. Jim Benefer's murder, both of them came out of Mrs. Emily Benefer's office together." "Did you notice anything suspicious about what Emily or Susan was doing or carrying in their hand?" "Yes, Emily had a syringe in her hand each time." Celeste looked at Judge Lanier, and said, "I have no further questions for this witness."

Judge Richard Lanier looked at the defense attorney, and said, "Is there any cross-examination Mr. Reed?" "No, your Honor."

"I call Mrs. Susan Janice Simmons to the stand."

"Mrs. Simmons, when you and Mrs. Benefer went into Mrs. Benefer's office at the restaurant on the two occasions that Mrs. Powell stated that she saw you go in earlier, what was the 'nature of your conversation?'" "It was just friendly, casual talk like we always had when we were together." "Why was Mrs. Benefer holding a syringe in her hand each time when she came out of her office?" "I do not know," said Mrs. Simmons.

Mr. Reed quickly interrupted, and said, "The syringe has no bearing on this case. Judge Lanier said to Celeste, "Keep your questions relevant to this case." Celeste looked toward Judge Lanier, and said, "With the court's permission, I plan to prove that the syringe was used in the murders of all three men.

Judge Lanier looked toward Mr. Reed, and said, "Overruled." Celeste continued her questioning of Mrs. Simmons. "Mrs. Simmons, it has been pointed out in earlier testimony that a syringe was used to inject poison into the food that killed Mr. Zetterower. Would you like to elaborate on what was in the syringe to kill, not only Mr. Randy Zetterower, but also Mr. Jim Benefer, and Doctor King?"

Susan said, "There was a poison substance in each syringe. That is all I know about it."
I have one more question for you, Mrs. Simmons. Were you the one who put Rhonda in the freezer to freeze to death?" "Yes, I

did it," said Susan. "That is all I have for this witness," said Celeste.

Judge Richard Lanier looked at the defense attorney, and said, "Is there any cross-examination Mr. Reed?" "No, your Honor."

Notes:

Celeste had talked to Susan before the trial. She told her that if she testified against Mrs. Benefer and tell the truth that she was the one who put Rhonda in the restaurant freezer that she would be able to reduce her involvement in the three murders to a lesser charge of five years in prison and two years probation rather than seven years in prison and three years probation.

"I call Doctor Grindle to the stand."

Then Celeste began the questioning session by a statement. "Doctor Grindle, the State of New York Crime Lab obtained a search warrant to go into the kitchen, backrooms, and Emily's office of 'Emily's Steak and Pizza House' on Tuesday last week. Since the three men were murdered by poisoning in the restaurant the crime lab team was looking for any type of poison substance in the area. When they went into Emily's office, one of the men discovered powder remains of a poison just under the edge of Emily's file cabinet. The person who cleaned her office failed to completely get all of the remains of the poison substance. Without saying anything to anyone in the area, the crime lab took samples back with them to the lab to compare it to that which was found in the bodies of the three men who were murdered."

Celeste continued by asking a question regarding her previous statement, and said, "Have you been to the New York Crime Lab and examined the poison that was found in Mrs. Benefer's office at Emily's Steak and Pizza House?" "Yes, I have." "Have you also seen a report from the New York State

Coroner who did an autopsy on Mr. Randy Zetterower, Mr. Jim Benefer, and Doctor King's bodies showing that poison was in their system?" "Yes." "Is the poison found at the restaurant the same as that which was found by the State of New York Crime Lab in the bodies of all three men?" "Yes, it was the same," said Doctor Grindle.

Notes:

After Doctor Grindle told the court that the poison which killed all three men was the same poison that was found in the restaurant, he also presented additional evidence against Emily through Doctor King's notes and his testimony. As Doctor Grindle made these final statements, Emily looked over toward Susan. Emily had the look on her face as if to say that she could not believe the State of New York Crime Lab had found remains of the poison in her restaurant.

Earlier on the day the New York Crime Lab, discovered the poison in her office, Emily had to momentarily go to another part of the restaurant's back room area to quickly take care of a problem with one of her waitresses. So, she did not know that they had found it.

Celeste enters Doctor King's second envelope as 'Exhibit 'J.'

With the court's permission, I would like to enter this second envelope that Doctor King's wife, Mary gave us earlier; but due to reasons that Judge Lanier and I discussed before the second trial it could not be entered as evidence until now. Celeste placed the envelope on a table in front of Judge Lanier's bench.

Then Celeste walked back to the witness stand, looked at Doctor Grindle, and said, "Dr Grindle, do you remember the second envelope that we obtained from Mrs. Mary King? Yes, I do. We could not enter the note in it as evidence until now due to the severe nature of the allegation.

Celeste walked back over to the table where she had placed the second envelope, picked it up, opened it, gave the note in it to Doctor Grindle, and said, "Doctor Grindle would you please read what this note says?" Doctor Grindle took the note in his hand. He looked at the note as he read it. Doctor Grindle said, "According to the note, Doctor King said that Jim Al Benefer told him Randy's murderer was Emily Mae Benefer. Everybody in the court began to talk among themselves. Judge Lanier said, "Order in the court."

Then, Celeste put the note back in the envelope and placed the envelope back on the table where she had picked it up before Doctor Grindle read the note in it.

"Is there any cross-examination Mr. Reed?"
"No, your Honor."

Notes:

This was also where Doctor Grindle tells about Emily's name being in the second envelope which he could not mention earlier at the second trial because they did not have enough evidence against Emily at that time to convict her ...even though Jim had stated that she was the one who murdered Randy.

The evidence is against her

When all of the evidence pointed to Mrs. Emily Benefer poisoning Randy, Jim, and Doctor King, no one could believe that she did it.

Celeste talks to the jury
Celeste told the jury <u>why</u> Mrs. Benefer poisoned each of the three men
Why was <u>Randy</u> murdered?
Why was Jim murdered?
Why was Doctor King murdered?

Mrs. Emily Benefer wanted to get rid of Randy so that she could marry Jim when Jim got out of prison.

Mrs. Emily Benefer he wanted to get rid of Jim because he told Doctor King that Emily murdered Randy and Jim.

When Mrs. Emily Benefer knew that Jim was going to testify against her in Randy's murder, she poisoned him. Jim was going to blame Mrs. Benefer in his testimony.

Mrs. Emily Benefer wanted to get rid of Doctor King because he was going to the local law enforcement authorities with what Jim had told him …and would probably testify against her in court.

Guilty beyond a reasonable doubt

Celeste had enough evidence against Mrs. Emily Benefer to know 'beyond a reasonable doubt' that she murdered all three men by using poison to kill them.

The verdict from the jury

After three major trials, the verdict is reached by the Jury.

The jury returns from the 'Jury Room.' After all twelve of the jurors sit down, Judge Lanier said, "Has the jury reached a verdict?" Mrs. Beverly Starkey, the spokesperson for the jury said, "We have your honor. We find the defendant Emily Mae Zetterower, guilty on three counts of first degree murder."

Celeste, Courtney, and Emily's third husband, Mr. Jesse Lee Wilbanks, were all in tears. As Celeste turned and looked toward Courtney, she said, "I'm sorry...

...but it had to be done.

Emily is taken away back <u>to jail</u>
Emily receives the <u>death penalty</u>
Then she was put on <u>death row</u>

Courtney cannot believe what Celeste has done

Courtney and Carol McDora went back to their separate homes and to their husbands with deep feelings of hurt and dismay. Both of them were having difficulty dealing with the death penalty verdict decision.

Mr. Jesse Lee Wilbanks went back home with feelings of hurt and loss that could not be described. He felt that things would never be the same again for him when Emily was gone on the day that she was sentenced to die by 'lethal injection.'

All three visited Emily on death row until the day of her fateful death by 'lethal injection.' That day was a sad day because not only was she going to die on the table that she was tied to when they injected her with the fatal chemical, but it took her twenty minutes to die as her body squirmed for someone to help her. She could not help herself as she was dying, and no one else would be able to help her either. Within minutes her body was still. It was all over. Good bye, Emily.

Celeste had solved the murder case when the police could not
It was hard on her, but she had to do it

She was guilty, too

Susan knew Emily. She worked with Emily in the restaurant and was Emily's confidant. Therefore, she knew that Emily was the murderer of all three men. Before Emily murdered Jim and Doctor King, Susan gave Emily information about how they were going to let someone know that Emily was the murderer. As noted earlier, since Susan was involved in the murders indirectly and because she testified against Mrs. Benefer, she was tried in a separate court of law and sentenced to five years in prison and two years probation rather than seven years in prison and three years probation.

The End

Larry V. Johnson

Her Love Did Not Change With What Had To Be Done

Larry V. Johnson

Made in the USA
Columbia, SC
24 September 2023